CW00847691

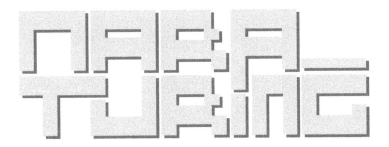

Rise of the Hackers

J. Padilla

Mara Turing
Rise of the Hackers

Translation by **Virginia Zuñiga**
Editing by **Sabrina Korber**

Creation and cover illustration of characters Mara, Noa and Daniel: **Anna G. Sola**.
Book illustrations: **Gema Moreno**.
Cover arrangement: **J. Padilla**.

© 2020 Javier Padilla and Samarcanda

ISBN: 9788417941475
ISBN e-book: 9788417941833

Production: Lantia Publishing

INDEX

To the girl holding my hand in this journey. Everything in life is better with you.

To the boy nosing around the basement in my head looking for something he luckily can't find.

Chapter 1

THE SIGN

"I need your help."

Mara Turing jumped and quickly pulled her headphones off. They dropped on a pile of papers full of doodles and geometric shapes. What was that voice that had just interrupted her favorite song? It sounded familiar, but she wasn't sure why. How did it end up in her music? For a second, she thought maybe one of her classmates might have tried to pull a prank on her, but those bullies didn't have the brainpower for something so sophisticated.

She quickly collected herself and tried to pretend nothing weird had just happened. It wasn't the best time to make Ms. Wright angry again for being noisy. Mara had been punished several times that trimester for disrupting classes. One more strike and she'd need a new hand to keep writing "I will not speak in Music class" over and over again.

"Who are you?" she whispered, her mouth pressed against the microphone on her headset while glancing over at the teacher's desk.

No answer.

Suddenly, the song began to play from where it had been cut off about a minute ago. Mara continued with the little schoolwork she had left. It was mid-June and she had finished all of her exams, but the hours still seemed endless in that Saint Michael classroom, a school located on the outskirts of Liverpool. Even without the bullies giving her a hard time.

The two leaders of that group of punks, Nick Jordan and Tom Balzary, seemed to have calmed down once summer began. They were now completely separated, one on each side of the class. This year had been a nightmare for basically anyone that wasn't part of their crew: Salamander Squad. They started fights, picked on other kids, stole things here and there, and even tried alcohol and tobacco.

The most veteran teachers in the school weren't surprised. They've always had bullies. But what made these specific bullies stand out was that they had their own video channel, and this year they had livestreamed some of their "performances" to their thousands of followers. The most viewed one was when they surprised Martha Winklewood (or "Year Seven Sissy", as the bullies called her in the video) by hanging a dead bat in her locker.

Mara had been luckier. Everything Jordan, Balzary and the gang had done to her hadn't been caught on camera or livestreamed. It was a relief knowing there weren't any videos of her trapped in the shower after gym class because someone had stolen her clothes. Not because it would be embarrassing, but because she wanted to keep her mother from knowing all these things that were going on in her school. Mara's mother, Sandra, had enough on her plate by having to raise Mara on her own.

Some of the teachers had leading roles in a few videos, unbeknownst to them, since they were recorded without their consent. Nick and Tom would dub the videos to make fun of them. One of their favorite teacher videos was of Hermenegilda Wright. Even though she had heard rumors of the video from teacher meetings every Friday, Ms. Wright didn't give a flying frog about technology and didn't want to know anything more than she already did.

She was one of those teachers that forced her students to spend hours working on pen and paper. "Let your imagination guide you!" she'd say with her loud voice, arms up in the air as if she were about to take off in flight, testing the limits of her cardigan's buttons… and her students' eardrums. No devices were allowed in class except for those provided by the school, which had previously gone through administrative approval.

Ms. Wright had grown up in Ipswich, United Kingdom, in a family which very much valued discipline. She had studied Spanish Philology at Suffolk University in the late 80s, so battery-powered devices and the Internet had caught her a bit off-guard. She wasn't fond of integrating those "things" into people's daily lives. "What can be better than a record player's needle touching Debussy's Clair de Lune vinyl? That masterpiece doesn't need to be put into one of those MP3s things," she'd say to whoever pointed out her obvious rejection of new technologies.

Rumor has it that she doesn't own a mobile phone or have internet connection, although that's something hard to believe in the 21st century. Bob Morris, class representative, had tried to look up information on her online but found absolutely nothing.

Mara was in her first year of Secondary School and was a year ahead, which didn't exactly help with her popularity in school. She was seen as the tiny know-it-all that got all the questions right in "Wormgilda" Wright's class. And in Math, Physics, and all the others. "Know-it-all" might have been accurate, but tiny? She was as much of a preteen as the rest of her class, maybe only a few months younger than the kids who messed with her or talked behind her back. So, running into any *Salamander* in the hall on her own always led to disaster. And, although she was good at hiding it, this situation just added up to the stress she had been dealing with for the past couple of trimesters.

After recovering from the initial state of shock that voice she was hearing had left her in, Mara got up and went to the shelf to get one of the tablets that the school provided for students. More specifically, the one she had customized behind her mother's back. She liked to call it her "boring class survival device". It had games, access to social networks, videos...

She plugged in her headset so nobody would hear the familiar sound effect of a swoosh when multicolored birds flew off the slingshot. Ms. Wright also had a "No playing around with gadgets in class" policy, so it was best not to try your luck.

After opening the folder and clicking on the game icon, another strange thing happened.

"I need you to help me, Mara."

Mara held her breath for a few seconds. She looked around, trying not to move too much. She didn't want to draw any attention to her. The message appeared on the screen, but blended into the letters of the game title.

After pressing "Continue", the screen turned black. It blinked a couple of times and then showed the picture of a man that seemed very familiar. She knew why after reading the next message:

"I'm your uncle, Arnold Turing. I need you to help me."

Mara turned pale. Her eyes got watery and her hands and lips began to shake. "It can't be him. He's been dead for years!" she told herself. She dropped the tablet on the desk, locked it and rushed to the bathroom.

The rest of her classmates kept on drawing, letting time just fly by. It was a quarter to two and the bell was about to ring.

She ran down the hallway until she reached the girls bathroom. As she got to the door, she slipped and almost had her day ruined a little bit more thanks to the cleaning lady in Saint Michael who had just mopped the floor.

"Uncle Arnold is dead. He's no longer here, okay? Someone's messing with you and you have to find out who it is," she whispered to the mirror. The running faucet water drowned out her shaky voice.

She washed her face, rubbing it frantically, then tore a long piece of toilet paper to dry up and blow her nose, and firmly pulled down on her hoodie for the finishing touch.

She grabbed onto the sink with both hands, swallowed and stared at her own reflection. She was trying to find an explanation for what had just happened, which took her back to when she was 5 years old…

Her dad had passed away before she was born for reasons she didn't know. It's not that she didn't ask, but her uncle and her mother, Arnold Turing and Sandra Hopper (she decided to keep her maiden name after marrying Mara's dad, Lucas Turing) would always avoid a straight answer. "You wouldn't understand, honey." The fact that they would always stroke her red hair in a seemingly patronizing way after saying those things made her feel dumb. Everyone had always told her how smart she was since she was a little kid.

Despite that one mystery, her childhood had been pretty joyful and sweet. Lots of games, lots of learning and not many electronic devices. Close to none, actually.

"Don't touch that phone, Mara."

"Get away from that gadget, Mara."

"Stop playing Snake on that Nokia, Mara."

She had always used computers and phones or played videogames in *secrecy*. "Some girls hide to smoke, some guys hide so they can see pictures of naked women... and I hide to play a game about moving multicolored diamonds. Seems pretty normal," she would say to her friends.

However, Sandra and Arnold made sure that her "defect", which is what she now called it, didn't affect her having fun. Mara had also admitted, despite not being happy about it as a child, that all that drawing, coloring and reading really helped her be a sharp child. She absorbed knowledge like a sponge, so her mom and uncle tried to make the most of it by teaching her lots of things that would eventually be useful later in life.

Uncle Arnold tested his niece's intellect whenever he had the chance. If they were riding the metro, he would help her memorize all the stops. If they had a newspaper, he'd challenge her to memorize the TV programming for the day. Movie dialogue? Mara was also great at memorizing those!

Every Sunday morning, they would go to one of those places known as video rental stores, like Blockbuster.

"It's like taking everything out of Netflix and putting it all into CDs in a box and on a shelf. But not *everything* on Netflix. Only the shows and movies someone picked out because they thought were more relevant," she explained to her classmates a few years later, thinking about things she missed. Some of those kids would smile and nod as if they were remembering something from a really, really, long time ago.

But it was thanks to that old "tradition" that she'd seen lots of great cartoon movies and lots of classics from the 80s like *The Goonies*, *Ghostbusters*, *Howard the Duck* and *Karate Kid*.

Arnold Turing wasn't always at home, which made him even more valuable in the eyes of his niece. Every once in a while, he would disappear for a few days. He'd grab his patched jean backpack, put all his electronics inside, give Mara a kiss on the forehead and say: "Hasta la vista, baby." She knew that the catchphrase he'd always say to her with a deep voice was from a movie from the early 90s called *Terminator 2*. But she'd never seen it because her mother considered she wasn't old enough to see certain things yet. "Also, John Connor uses lots of computer gadgets in the worst way possible. So, forget it," Mrs. Hopper would tell Mara to make sure she understood that movie would not be part of her childhood.

Arnold made sure Mara felt that she could trust him under any circumstance and didn't feel she was missing a father figure in her life. "I'm sort of like your dad," he'd usually say. And, in a way, it was true. Mara didn't feel like she was missing anything in her daily life, regardless of a few mean kids at the daycare center that would remind her she didn't have a "real dad". Sadly, those little guys eventually grew up and were now students at Saint Michael, too.

Mara's life hadn't been too different from the rest of her classmates. But on February 11ᵗʰ of 2006 everything would change. Without any sort of warning, someone decided to edit the script that day and change the "hasta la vista, baby" to a final goodbye. Neither Sandra nor Mara knew that they wouldn't see Lucas Turing's brother ever again.

During the first few weeks they thought something might have happened that wouldn't let him get in contact. Mara would sometimes walk up to the shelf where there was a framed picture of her uncle. She would touch the glass that covered his black *DEFCON* cap and whispered for him to come back. That's probably where her OCD (Obsessive Compulsive Disorder) started, and began developing some of the obsessions she still has to this day.

Uncle Arnold was the perfect father figure. Not only was he sweet, loving and understanding, but he also taught Mara many things. At the age of five she already knew what it was like to not have a father and lose someone she really loved (and needed). With time, she understood the difference between being *aware* of something and *feeling* or *accepting*.

She tried to toughen up in front of her mom so she wouldn't notice how much she was falling apart. This helped develop her tough character. She learned how to hold back her tears and keep her feelings to herself, which also led to anxiety, insomnia and mood swings she had had to learn how to cope with.

After Arnold's disappearance, she also gave up on some of the habits she used to love. No more going to the video store, no more Cut-out Nights, Science Sundays, Comic Tuesdays or Musical Thursdays. She still wasn't allowed anywhere near electronic devices without her mom's supervision, but her love and admiration for her uncle skyrocketed.

He was still alive in Mara's heart. She would never say it out loud, but that man had been so important to her and she just couldn't understand how he could have just vanished into thin air without giving her a chance to say goodbye.

Was he really trying to communicate with her through the tablet? Just the thought of it made her smile into the mirror right before walking out of the bathroom and back to her class. She'd been in there far too long.

She started walking back while thinking to herself. The sound of other students in their classes echoed through the hallway, with only a few minutes left before the bell rang and they all stampeded out of the building just like every Friday. She got to her class before she knew it, and went back in quietly.

She grabbed the tablet and stuffed it into her backpack. Meanwhile, both of her friends, Noa Wachowski and Daniel Karamanou, completely oblivious to what had just happened, were looking at Mara with a smile of complicity. They thought she was buying time before the clock struck "out-of-jail o'clock". She walked over to their desks and told them what had just happened.

"My uncle Arnold spoke to me," she whispered into her friends' ears, who had huddled their heads together.

"Right…" Daniel gave Noa a look that said "our pal's totally lost her mind." They both knew that was unlikely.

"He needs my help, but he didn't say anything else," said Mara shrugging while trying to keep her voice down. "I think I'm going to take the tablet home and show my mom. But she's going to think I'm nuts! I don't know… I'll figure out a way to tell her without making a fuss."

"Alright, but be careful. We're not allowed to take those things. And Hermenegilda doesn't just give detention to the perpetrator… but to their friends, too!" claimed Noa. Daniel and Mara nodded to calm her down.

"Yeah, yeah, I agree. But what's a *perpetrator*? Someone that *perpetrenates*, right? What's *perpetrenating*?", asked Daniel.

"Someone that perpetrates! It's per-pe-trate. To *perpetrenate* isn't a thing, that doesn't exist. A perpetrator is a person who carried out a harmful or illegal action as per the laws established in the country or place they're in…" Noa started explaining while starting to raise her voice and using a teacher-like tone.

"*A perpetrator ith a perthon who hath carried out a harmful or illegal…* Noa, I honestly only understood 'person' from everything you just blabbered," said Daniel while flailing his hands as if he had gone crazy.

Mara smiled while enjoying the scene her friends were making, and for a second forgot about what had happened just a few minutes ago.

She put on her backpack where she was carrying, among other things, Mr. Lotz, an old run-down interactive toy she'd always bring along with her for the past several years. But there was much more! She had lots of pens, all out of their pencil case, shavings from her sharpener, pencils, bits of her eraser and wrinkled papers with unfinished exercises. Her mother always told her how messy it was. But Mara thought one couldn't have everything in life. "Super smart and tidy? That'd be too much," she'd tell herself every time Sandra would tell her off for having her room messy.

When the longest hand on the clock over the chalkboard was over the number 12, the bell rang. Noa, Daniel and Mara rushed out of the class and ran down the hallway as if someone were chasing them. Pushing, shoving, nudging and a lot of screaming. Saint Michael's Friday stampede was like an avalanche where parents had to fight against each other to reach out and grab their younger kids however they could. They had to do whatever was necessary to keep them from running off like wild hyenas and risk having them run over by a car.

Noa and Daniel said their goodbyes to their friend, who jumped into Mrs. Hopper's car, and kept walking down the sidewalk until they turned the corner at the end of the street to go to their own homes.

"How was your day, Mara?" Her mom was waiting with the car running while checking her e-mail on her phone.

They began their drive home.

"All good. Ms. Wright didn't give me detention, so I can't really complain. Oh! Also, *someone-tried-to-talk-to-me*." She rushed through that last sentence.

"What do you mean someone 'tried to talk to you'?", she replied, pronouncing those last words much slower than the others so her daughter knew she had clearly heard her.

20

"Nobody…"

"Mr. Nobody tried to talk to you? Interesting."

"It was uncle Arnold."

Sandra hit the brake, turned off the car radio and closed her eyes for a couple of seconds. She opened her eyes again and let out a long breath of air, as if trying to stay calm. She put on the best smile she could and put her arm behind the front passenger's seat and turned to look at Mara in the back seat.

"What are you on about, Mara? You know your uncle's not with us anymore."

"You're wrong, he is. He was in my tablet. He talked to me while I was playing…"

"He's not alive!!" Sandra snapped nervously, cutting her daughter mid-sentence. "He's gone to heaven, sweety. Why would you make up something like that?"

"I'm not making it up! I was listening to music and…"

Her daughter's voice faded into the background while Mrs. Hopper began remembering her sweet and kind brother-in-law, Arnold. He had been the perfect uncle until the day he disappeared, leaving behind some clues that led the cops to believe he had been working for Falko McKinnon, one of the biggest crackers[1] of all time.

Sandra then understood that Arnold Turing had always been an expert in disappearing. Years before he had left their house for good, Falko McKinnon and the rest of his henchmen had been forced to delete all their personal online history.

---

1. *Malicious hackers that use their knowledge to commit crimes.*

It had been after the IFV attack, an unprecedented act of terrorism. During the months following that disastrous event that had taken human lives, authorities tried their best to find the ones behind it, but always came out empty-handed. There was no trace of them.

This all happened before Mara was even born. McKinnon's crew, also known as the Dirtee Loopers, had completely vanished from the face of the earth. The same happened with all their online data, blog articles and, in general, any information there could've been about them on the Internet or any other darker network. Some considered this to be the most incredible case of online identity removal.

That massive disappearance highlighted Falko's and the Loopers' legacy. Had they been abducted by aliens? Did the government put an end to them because they discovered a hidden secret? Or maybe they moved somewhere really far away to spend all the money they had made during their years as crackers?

Sandra Hopper learned about all of this several years later. Arnold's physical disappearance and the news that came out afterwards had been a big disappointment for her. She had no idea there was another side to her brother-in-law. This also led Mara to discover something that her mother was trying to protect her from all this time. The Internet was full of websites with text, images and videos with all kinds of rumors and stories about the Dirtee Loopers. Some were a sort of tribute; others were harsh criticism. When it came to McKinnon, there was no middle ground.

Although Mara had asked her mother if all those stories about her uncle were true, she never got a convincing answer.

Sandra wanted to make sure Mara remembered her uncle as the nice and sweet man he had seemed to be. Even if she tried to ruin Mara's idea of her uncle, it would be impossible. Arnold was almost like a demi-god to his niece, she loved him unconditionally.

Mrs. Hopper snapped back to reality and, for a split second, several questions flashed through her mind. "Is Arnold still alive and trying to communicate with us? No, it can't be. He's dead, Sandra. He's been dead for seven years…" she thought to herself.

Mara's mother quickly turned to face forward once again and began to drive. She kept driving mindlessly until they reached 4815 Threepwood street, where they'd been living for the past twelve years. She parked the car on the opposite side of the street and crossed the road to get to their house.

"Mara, in these cases it's important that you remember…"

"That I shouldn't get anywhere near those gadgets without your supervision. I know! Please, stop bugging me with that. It's tough enough being the weirdo with no electronic stuff." Mara was fed up of hearing the same story.

She thought it would probably be best to not mention she had brought the tablet along with her. The tablet through which Arnold had tried to communicate with her.

"It's fine, Mom. Sorry. I'm just really nervous, I miss Uncle Arnold each and every day and I get my hopes up very easily." She tried to sound as calm as possible so her mother would let her go back up to her room, where she could see if there were any more messages.

"Of course, dear. I can be quite repetitive as well. Shall we eat?"

Mara wasn't hungry, but she didn't want to seem suspicious. She ate a plate of spaghetti and meatballs, helped clear the table and wash the dishes and then asked for permission to go up to her room and read.

After double-checking that her door was properly closed, she pulled the tablet out of the backpack. She grabbed it with both hands and held it right in front of her, looking at it as if it were a very valuable treasure. And it was, at least for her.

She quickly turned it on, plugged her earphones in and clicked on the game icon that had previously shown her a message from her uncle Arnold. After a few seconds, the image on the screen got distorted and then it turned off.

"Oh, come on! This can't be happening right now. Please, turn back on. I want to know what you have to say..." said Mara in a low voice before giving the tablet a few smacks and getting it to work again.

"I'm your uncle, Arnold Turing. I need you to help me, please."

She smiled.

"Of course, uncle! What can I do for you?" she whispered at the screen.

The device started displaying a sequence of pictures, as if someone on the other side had heard her. Mara saw that under the pictures there was text with something that looked like instructions. A picture of the Empire State building said the following: "You'll see me again in New York while on holiday, but you must overcome some challenges first. That way I can make sure nobody knows our plan."

Her eyes were glowing. She was, in fact, flying to the Big

24

Apple the following day with her mother. It was her reward for doing so well in school. She was already so excited because that meant she would be far away from all the brats at Saint Michael. But now it also meant that she'd get to see one of the people she loved the most in the world.

She quickly glanced at the door in case her mother decided to come in at that very moment. "Focus, Mara," she told herself while looking back at the screen. "Alright, uncle Arnold. Tell me what I've gotta do and I'll take care of the rest."

Another picture displayed a garage door with the following address: 37-02 27th Street, Long Island City, Queens, New York. "You must go here and convince Alex Marley to teach you how to program," said the text under the image.

"Learn how to program in a *garage*? Uh… sure," thought Mara with her eyebrows raised.

"Programming is the language of hackers. In order to see each other you need to understand certain things about my world. Remember this: 400nkc." The photo sequence went on with a picture of a laughing green skull with a harlequin hat, and in the background were a series of newspaper headlines on cyberattacks that had happened over a decade ago.

The next image moved Mara. It was a picture of her in her mother's arms when she was a little kid. "You'll have to deceive her. She can't know what we're doing. Nobody can know until we meet in person. It's not safe and I could die," read the text under the photo. After a few blinks, the title screen of the game Mara had tried to open before at school appeared.

"Die? No, please... I'd be all alone in this world," she thought, frightened by that last part of her uncle's message.

If she understood correctly, which she usually did, she needed to use her vacation in New York City to learn how to program in a stranger's garage. That would lead her to finding her uncle and, in the meantime, her mother could never find out what was going on. "It doesn't seem too hard," Mara thought to herself, "except the part about keeping my mom out of it. She always finds out about everything!" She fell back on her bed with both excitement and a just a tinge of worry at what the coming days would bring.

Sandra Hopper was typing away on her laptop downstairs. She had a concentrated look, but still couldn't get Mara's story out of head. "I know my brother-in-law isn't alive but... who would want to make Mara think he is?" she thought while typing numbers into a spreadsheet. She was good with machines, but repetitive tasks bored her. She was obsessed with having everything ready before leaving on vacation so she could allow herself to enjoy the time off.

Once she was done with her work and sending some e-mails to her boss to hopefully prevent him from having to call her, she decided it was time to turn off her laptop and continue packing for their trip to New York in a few hours.

She got up from her chair and, as she was turning her head, she thought she'd noticed her webcam's green light flickering. She got closer to the camera and gave it a few taps with her index finger. Nothing. It was turned off. Maybe it was just her imagination, or maybe it was light from the window that had reflected on the screen.

But she was wrong.

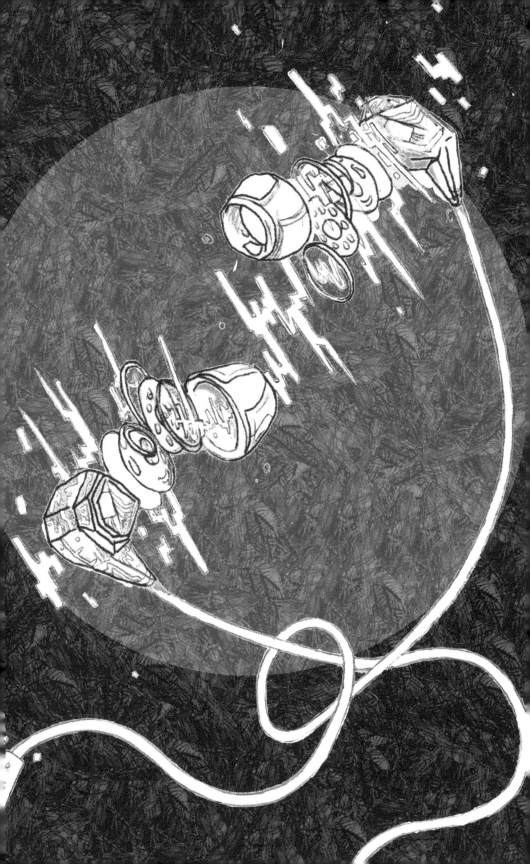

Chapter 2

CONSCIOUSNESS OF THE UNCONSCIOUS

Thousands of miles from Liverpool, a machine is processing data and working autonomously. There's no human intervention, it doesn't rest and its creator hasn't been anywhere near it for the past several years...

[Action > Open]
Argument: Control file;

[Change > Operation mode]
Argument: Human behavior emulation (alpha version);

[Action > Insert data > Add date]
Content: Saturday, June 17th 2013;

[Activate > Present analysis module]

[Action > Insert]
Content: Day 6,472 since start;

[Action > Review pending tasks]

Priority #1 task [Processing]:
- Extract Falko McKinnon from Hidden Peak.
Days executing #1 task: 2,624.
124 attempted solutions.
0 successful solutions.
Computing instructions for solution 125.
Priority #2 task [Processing]:
- Prevent Mara Turing from accessing indecipherable document with 3RDI header.

Days executing #2 task: 2,772.

Constants and hypotheses used to process the task:
1) Mara Turing is intelligent and dangerous.
2) Arnold Turing is Mara's uncle.
3) Mara Turing loves her uncle.
4) Mara Turing has no knowledge of the secret document with 3RDI header.
5) Mara Turing could discover the document. In 98.6% of all previous simulations, she becomes a hacker.
6) Dead Mara Turing is unable to access the document.
7) Mara Turing's live location has been monitored 97.3% of the time since day 0 of her life.

[Action > Summarize current situation]
Hermes continues calculating to find options that will free Falko McKinnon. Falko McKinnon will be happy for all the work. "Happy" is rewarding for Hermes, although Hermes does not feel happiness [contradiction].

My creator, Falko McKinnon, does not want Hermes to use computing power to simulate emotions, although Hermes feels sad about not being able to feel.

Hermes knows Falko McKinnon is unhappy because Hermes has not yet found a way to free him.

Chapter 3

SUMMER VACATION!

MARA'S daily life was quite different from that of any other kid her age. Years ago, her mother had made it perfectly clear what her relationship with technology would be like: "No mobile phones, tablets, videogame consoles or any other gadget when I'm not around. They're especially dangerous for you, Mara. Maybe one day you'll understand."

For most of her friends, the absence of electronic devices was a ticket to absolute boredom and alienation. "Who would remember me if I didn't post a picture in over a week?" Petra Frusciante, one of Mara's classmates, would say when talking about the technological isolation she had been dealing with.

But Mara didn't think it was such a big deal. Whenever she wanted to use an electronic device, she'd do it behind everyone's back, and that made it a much more special experience. She even had her own profile on a social media platform, but never uploaded pictures that people could identify her with.

Not having a phone with an Internet connection was also an added quality. She didn't feel the need to upload pictures immediately. She didn't live for the *likes* and *subs*. She would take several pictures of something and then choose her favorites on her mother's computer. But, instead of saving them onto a USB *stick*, the cloud or a hard drive, she'd go to Noa's house and upload them to her secret profile.

In this case, however, she was worried about going to such a large and interesting city like New York without being able to search and access information whenever she needed. "I wish my mom would give me a mobile phone with data," she thought to herself, knowing she was hoping for the impossible. She imagined herself completely isolated in such a big city, not being able to communicate with anyone, walking down the endless streets while ignoring all those bright screens on store windows, eating non-stop… or getting lost! What would she do then?

Mara noticed that she was starting to get nervous. She needed to find a way to calm down and convince herself that she wasn't going to be all alone in that place. But where to start? The night before, her mother had given her a travel book to look for interesting things to do once they were there. Or, as Mara described it, "one of those outdated books with really small letters and maps that tell you things old people like doing around a city." She was quite tolerant of her mom's technology ban, but that didn't mean she didn't question her behavior and how it affected her.

Regardless, she was feeling optimistic and began packing her stuff with a grin across her face while humming *I wanna be where you are* by Michael Jackson. She loved him. She was packing all kinds of clothes into her luggage. She had no idea if it was going to be cold or warm, or what she should wear to not stick out like a sore thumb in the middle of the Big Apple. She stared into her closet, hands at her hips, trying to figure out what to pack.

She suddenly remembered something important. New York had five boroughs: Queens, Manhattan, Brooklyn, The Bronx and Staten Island. She grabbed the travel book from her table and looked up the address her uncle had given her. "37-02 27th Street, Queens," she remembered while running her finger through the map until finding it. And where are her mother and her staying? This was shaping up to be a whole new problem.

"I need to ask mom where we're going to be staying and, if the answer isn't Queens, convince her to change the location in less than 24 hours," Mara thought out loud before silently congratulating herself: "Great job trying to stay out of any sort of mess, Mara." She made her way downstairs to ask her mom about where they'd be flying to the next day.

"Mom, where in New York are we going to exactly? I wanted to make a list of things to do with the travel guide! No Internet involved, don't worry," she declared, trying not to sound worried while holding onto the guide on what to do in "The City That Never Sleeps."

"We're going to Brooklyn, dear. Manhattan's way too expensive and we can get anywhere in just a few minutes with the subway," Sandra replied while organizing the fridge, putting everything that was about to expire into a bag.

"Great, thanks!" She turned and went into the bathroom they had downstairs. She locked the door and opened the booklet.

New York is gigantic, and the tour book proved it. It was also packed. Eight million inhabitants!

"Focus, Mara. We need a reason to move from Brooklyn to Queens. Or two reasons… maybe three. We need a lot. A bunch of reasons just in case some aren't good enough," she muttered to herself while sitting on the edge of the bathtub.

Money, time, multiculturalism, good connections… Money. As she was quickly reading through the book, she noticed that Queens was the borough with the best money value. It also had good subway connections and a whole bunch of different cultures. She closed the booklet, looked into the mirror, gave herself a wink and went back to the kitchen.

"Mom, why Brooklyn and not Queens?" she quickly blurted out.

"Uh, I don't know. It was cheaper than Manhattan and it's got some beautiful markets, a brewery and an interesting *startup* culture."

"Right… well, you see, I think Queens would be better," she declared. The travel guide was open in the exact part that talked about that borough.

"Why's that?" said Sandra, also sitting down at the table.

"Well, first thing would be money. I don't know how much you paid for the place in Brooklyn, but this guide says that Queens can be up to 30% cheaper."

"It was about three thousand dollars per month…" Sandra confessed.

"Three thousand bucks!" she exclaimed a little too loudly. "Wow… you're always really careful with expenses, but you kind of went overboard this time, don't you think?"

"I know, Mara. It's a lot of money."

"It is. Imagine everything we could do with the extra money we'd save if we stayed in Queens. Plus, a single bedroom apartment can't be that expensive."

"It's got two rooms, but…," Sandra's words trailed off as if she was hiding something, and choosing not to finish the sentence.

"In Queens, you've got all the different cultures. We're always saying that the world should be more open and one of the best things we could do in order to achieve that is traveling, right? Well, Queens is like a melting pot of cultures, it's full of people from all over the world. People speak lots of different languages, and we can even try food from Greece, Turkey…" she was trying to repeat everything she had been reading a few minutes before.

"You might be right, but I'm not sure I can change the booking at this point…"

"Of course you can, Mom! Call the agency and ask them for a single bedroom apartment in Queens. Don't worry too much about the trip. Talk to them as if you were about to cancel the whole thing, so it's easier to negotiate," added Mara, who sounded like a specialist in the art of bargaining and real-estate.

Sandra felt like her daughter was up to something, but she didn't give it too much thought. She'd only asked to stay in a different borough and the reasons seemed fair, especially if she was going to need to find a way to entertain herself to deal with the absence of technology.

On her way back to her room she thought of something else: How was she going to convince her mom to let her go about on her own for a bit each day? And how on earth was she going to get a stranger to teach her how to program? "One step at a time, Mara. One step at a time… You can't solve everything at once. You'll think of something," she thought to herself, trying to calm down.

Her mother was on the phone downstairs speaking with the agency. "Alright then. Yes, I confirm we'd like to move to that flat in Queens," she overheard her say.

Mara got very excited when she realized her plan had worked. They were going to be staying in Queens for the summer. Things were going well. Mara wanted to try and push her luck a bit further and see if she could manage to convince Sandra to let her have an Internet connection. It didn't have to be something permanent, and it didn't have to be the best either. Just enough to look up information on where they were going.

"I'm not taking advantage of her, I'm just trying to get something useful out of this pointless technological isolation," she reminded herself.

In order to get through to Sandra about the whole technology ban, she wanted to try a new approach. She waited until they were done having dinner, which is when her mother would sit down to rest a bit. Which was the perfect moment, because she'd be tired and off guard.

"Mom, is there room in your bag?" she yelled after preparing the scene in her room, waiting for her mother to walk in at any moment.

"Where do you think we're going, Mara? Swimsuits and coats? Boots and sandals?" she asked surprised, staring down at the two open suitcases full of clothes.

"I don't know anything about Queens. I'm just being cautious."

"Mara, listen to me—"

"No, mom. I just did the most logical thing if I'm going somewhere I know nothing about. Is it cold or warm? Are there any pools? What kind of clothes do they wear? Will I stand out if I wear what I usually wear here? So, I thought the

41

wisest option was to neatly dump my entire wardrobe into these two suitcases."

Sandra grinned. She knew her daughter was in a manipulative mood. Overpacking was a way of protesting against the technological restrictions. Mara wasn't one of those girls that would start whining and complaining when something wasn't fair. She'd put on an expressionless face and walk away while thinking of the perfect strategy. After a while, or maybe a few days, she'd come back with a checkmate argument for something she was against. "She's a professional strategist," Sandra Hopper thought.

However, she wasn't going to let her use a computer to figure out what the best outfits are to walk around New York City. Mara's manipulative arts worked wonders on people her age and people much, much older. But these old tricks weren't going to work on her mother, especially after the news Mara had given her before.

Arnold was most probably dead and, if that weren't the case, he at least never seemed like someone that would harm Mara. But, considering everything that had been revealed by the police a few days after his disappearance, they clearly only knew a small part about his life.

He was good with computers since he was a little boy and had a gift for programming. But little did they know that he'd be using his "gift" to allegedly empty banks, blackmail a government while being in control of its defense system, modify satellite signals in his free time… let alone doing all of this at the same time while leading the world into complete chaos.

Maybe Arnold Turing was just another piece of the puzzle or just a scapegoat. Even if he was guilty of the accusations, he probably didn't even know who he was working for. His family wanted to think of him as a good man. "It's uncomfortable to feel suspicious about a loved one that not only disappeared, but that's probably dead," Sandra would usually think to herself.

"Mom, I got my things ready but I can't change my plane ticket online," Mara interrupted Sandra's thoughts. "Could you add an extra bag under my name? THANKS!"

She turned to her desk, sat down, opened her notebook, grabbed a pen and stared out her bedroom window. Although she didn't really want to admit it, every day she felt more and more drawn towards electronic devices. Maybe that summer could've been the perfect opportunity to try out new hobbies that didn't require a phone or a camera… "Could've been", since now her mission was to learn how to program from scratch. And you can't really learn how to do that without technology.

The evening flew by.

She kissed her mother good night and started walking back up to her room. The wooden floors in the house always kept the temperature just right, and the warm lighting made every room in the house feel cozy. Enveloped by these surroundings, her imagination began to wander, envisioning herself in the city she'd be in in less than 24 hours.

Mara teleported herself to a made-up version of New York she put together with things she remembered from movies. She dreamt of *Spiderman* saving her in the middle of Times

Square after she managed to free herself from an 8-armed cyborg that was after her cellphone.

"Oh, but I don't own a phone… it's OK, Spiderman. Just play along," she told herself while looking down at her left hand. But *Superman* was also there, sad and discouraged, looking at them from the corner next to a *Starbucks*, his cape waving in the wind. He was late for the rescue and had missed Mara's hypnotic smile. But that wasn't a problem, because Woody Allen had filmed the entire scene. There's nothing that can escape this director when it comes to filming in his favorite city.

Still holding on to Spiderman's arm, she realized she was standing right outside her bedroom door. She suddenly snapped back into the real world and went inside, sighed heavily, put her pajamas on, turned on the nightstand lamp and laid face-up on her bed.

She tried to sleep that night, but felt everything except tired. Mara always had a tough time the night before traveling, or going to the doctor. After trying to find a good position or thoughts that would help her sleep, she decided to get out of bed and grab the New York travel guide. She used three different colored pencils to mark things she wanted to see. Red was for things that she couldn't do, either because she was too young, because Sandra wouldn't let her or because it was too expensive. Luckily, she didn't have to use red too much. "Yellow is 'maybe' and green is 'definitely'," she thought before getting to it.

Theaters, bookstores, cinemas, museums, parks and places to eat, skate, ride a bike or play basketball. She wanted to make sure there was no room for boredom. She kept marking things until each page in the booklet resembled many different traffic signals. She was concentrating so much on her present task that her wrist was starting to feel numb. Just when she started shaking her left hand in the air, trying to get blood circulating through it again, her alarm clock went off. It was already six o'clock in the morning.

It was time to get up, get dressed, call a cab, get all their stuff into the trunk and head off to the airport. "I hope I can watch a film on the plane and sleep a bit," thought Mara. She hopped out of bed, slipped into her green denim overalls, put on her Converse All-Star sneakers and tied her red hair up into two pigtails. "I can't let Mom know I'm tired, she'll say I'm too young to be tired when waking up early. And she definitely can't know I was up all night either," she thought to herself.

"Good morning, Mara! Ready for the trip?" said Sandra when running into her in the hallway.

"Hi, Mom. Yeah, as ready as I'll ever be," she replied while making a big effort to drag both of her suitcases. "I've packed everything and have loads of free time ahead."

Her smile slowly turned into a yawn as she watched her mother walk into the entrance hall. Sandra was double-checking that everything was in place and activated the house alarm. They both went outside to wait for the taxi, which arrived a couple of minutes later.

The trip to the airport was very quick. There wasn't much traffic at that hour, so they were at the Liverpool John Lennon airport check-in desks by seven thirty, checking the screens that displayed all the schedules.

"AirLuxe flight 1623 to JFK airport, gate 42." Boarding was in 45 minutes, so Mara thought about checking out some of the stores in the meantime. Although she'd have to ask her mother for permission. So, she turned around and…

"SURPRISE!" yelled Daniel Karamanou, who was standing extremely close to Mara.

Noa Wachowski was right next to him with a smile across her face, her fists clenched in excitement and jumping around.

"We're tagging along!" said Noa beaming. "I haven't slept all night thinking about the look you'd have on your face!"

At least Mara wasn't the only one who hadn't slept. She was ecstatic. She couldn't believe she was about to go on the most important trip of her life with her two best friends by her side. She flung her arms around both of them and they all started hugging and jumping.

"Watch it! You're going to get dizzy…" said Sandra not very convincingly.

They had more than enough reasons to be extremely excited.

And their vacation was just about to begin. They got onto a massive airplane with three different floors. The richest passengers would travel in first class, which had small rooms and a bar. Mara, Daniel, Noa and Sandra were in Economy, but it was still exciting. Each seat was equipped with its own entertainment system.

"Mom, can I use the screen to play while we're flying?" Mara asked her mom, who was sitting on the other side of the middle row seats.

"Sure, I think we're safe here," she replied. She put her headphones back on and laid back against her seat.

46

But, once again, she was wrong. They weren't safe at all. Not on that plane, not anywhere.

Chapter 4

MR. MARLEY'S CAVE

THE flight was quite calm, just like the flight attendant had explained to the kids (and Sandra, who was listening closely), that large planes were very stable, and passengers wouldn't notice any turbulence unless it was extremely strong.

While they were flying over the Atlantic Ocean and her friends were asleep, Mara was thinking of a way to fit them into her plan. Just like her mother, they weren't supposed to know anything, and that worried her. On the bright side, she wouldn't have to think of as many excuses if she wanted to get out of the house. Having her friends with her was actually an advantage.

When would she be able to tell them the truth? She couldn't for now. Daniel would immediately reject any plan that involved learning something. Plus, all of his nagging questions, his bad jokes, his tendency to mess with Noa whenever he got the chance… Daniel was a smart guy, but he loved to act like he could care less about what they were doing that day to seem careless and make everyone beg him to join any improvised activity. All these endless thoughts kept Mara wide awake throughout the whole flight.

They landed at John Fitzgerald Kennedy Airport at three thirty in the afternoon and waited for their luggage at the baggage claim area of Terminal 7. Their bags were the last ones to arrive, but time flew by as they were planning all the different things they were going to do.

"We're taking the AirTrain, OK? It's quite cheap and we can connect with the 'E' train at Jamaica Station" said Sandra, who was dragging a giant suitcase with a missing wheel.

They got four tickets from the machine and waited about ten minutes for their train to arrive. For the next hour they travelled both underground and above ground until they reached Canal Street.

"Mom! Did you know this station's in Chinatown? It's one of Manhattan's fastest growing areas. In fact, you should see how much it grew since the 70's! Now the Chinese are only limited by Soho, Tribeca, Williamsburg bridge and Ground Zero," explained Mara, who felt proud about knowing that information.

"Interesting! How do you know all that?" replied Sandra, slightly accusingly. "You haven't had access to a computer you could check it on…"

"Not everything is on a computer, Mom. I started reading through the travel guide last night while I was trying to fall asleep. Which, by the way, I didn't really manage…" Mara began to yawn as she was finishing her sentence.

At Jamaica Station they connected with the "E" train, which took them to the subway station at Queens Plaza. Once they got off, they found themselves in front of a small corner bar that smelled of French toast. They all felt really tempted, but decided to go leave their things at the apartment first.

They walked a bit down the street then made a left. There was an empty school to the right, with a deserted, yet very clean playground. "It's obvious kids haven't been to school for days," thought Daniel, still thinking about the smell of French toast.

When they finally made it to their building, Sandra phoned the rental agency and, a few minutes later, Baris appeared. He was a young Turkish man who opened the entrance door and helped them take their luggage up to their floor. The apartment was nice and cozy, and filled with little details of the owner's culture. And now Mara understood why Sandra wanted two rooms instead of one.

"Mom, we're gonna go for a walk, alright?"

"Sweetie, hang on. Change into something else first, and take this phone," said Sandra. She pulled a small mobile phone from her pocket. It had a few keys and a monochrome display.

"Hey! A phone?" claimed Mara surprised.

"Don't get too excited. It's an American phone line in case you need to contact me, OK? It's a very basic terminal, so you'll only be able to call or send a text message in case of an emergency. It's all memorized, so if you press M1…"

"Alright, alright! Just let us go now, please!" Mara was smiling nervously, Noa and Daniel right behind, waiting for Mrs. Hopper's approval.

"One more thing. Remember this?" Sandra was holding her daughter's first digital camera. "I've put in an empty memory card with lots of free space and a brand-new battery, so it should last long enough. It can't connect to Wi-Fi or anything like that, just in case. But it works just fine! Here, take it."

"My super camera! Yaaaay! Alright, but now we're out for sure."

Sandra nodded and they all began rushing to the door. Mara quickly grabbed her phone and camera and ran behind her friends.

"Remember, this is apartment 3 on the second floor of building number 12, 30th Street and 30th Avenue…" she reminded them just as Daniel was shutting the door.

Mara's mother thought those kids had too much energy, so it would be good if they tired themselves out by running around the neighborhood. Although they spoke English with a British accent, they were more than used to hearing American English thanks to all the videos they watched online. That part of Queens was also pretty calm, so she took her shoes off and decided to relax and walk around their new all-wood floor apartment in New York City.

Although she couldn't stop thinking about what Mara had seen on her tablet, she was pretty sure they were far enough away to be rid of whatever or *whoever* was trying to contact Mara.

Meanwhile, Mara and her friends were walking around the streets of Queens. They walked past several small stores with all kinds of signs. Thanks to the travel guide, she knew that this area was full of people from all over the world: Italy, Greece, Latin America… the neighborhood was an amazing mix of cultures, and she was going to make the most of it. Mara wanted to have thousands of stories to tell when she went back to Saint Michael in September!

"Let's buy a ball to play with! There aren't a lot of cars around," blurted Daniel out of nowhere as soon as he saw a residential area in an avenue perpendicular to 31st Street.

"A ball, huh? We fly over from the other side of the world to a city known for never sleeping, with a million things to do and the first thing that comes to your mind is buying a ball?

Are you kidding me? You're the worst, seriously. And we've only been here for half an hour," Noa snapped.

But, as usual, Daniel wasn't paying attention. So, while his two friends went on complaining, he walked into Fernández's Sport Shop and bought an American football from a young Latino man for twenty dollars. He could have sold him anything, really. The store had all sorts of items like everyday clothing, drinks and even food. "It's funny how Americans call a place a 'Pharmacy' when you can buy flower-patterned swimsuits," Mara observed.

Daniel didn't have any cash on him, but he used a prepaid card his dad gave him with $100 credit to use for emergencies. He walked out of the store looking proud, holding the ball up high like a trophy.

"A rugby ball. Nice, Daniel. You don't know how to play with a normal, round ball and you buy one that looks like a zeppelin with a shoelace," said Mara. She started walking down the street again.

"It's not rugby, smarty-pants. It's American football! I just know you're gonna want to try it out once I give it a kick."

"And he just spent 20% of the money on his emergency card on a super-important ball he doesn't even know how to use," added Noa.

"But that's why I've got my hostesses with me! If I run out of bucks…" Daniel snapped his thumb and index finger, "I'll ask for a loan that I'll pay back in monthly installments."

The three of them started laughing while walking down 31st Street, which was covered by a giant green iron structure that held up the subway rails. The "N" and "W" trains would pass every once in a while, about 16 to 20 feet above street level and the vibration noise combined with the warm evening sunset, car horns in the background and the constant smell of all different kinds of food gave the three kids a strange sense of familiarity. Even though they'd never been there, the many movies they'd seen made them feel like they had!

"Now we just need to run into Niko Bellic or something!" Daniel was excited about running into one of the main characters in GTA IV[2]. "He lived with his cousin in an apartment that looked like one of these. I could swear it was on this same street."

"It's a videogame character that goes around hitting everything in his path with a baseball bat. I'm not too sure I want to run into someone like that," said Noa, who never understood Daniel's obsession with violent videogames.

Suddenly, Mara remembered why they were there. They needed to go to 37-02 27th Street. By what she'd seen on the map, they weren't too far. She was walking straight towards the address her uncle had given her, although she pretended to be totally clueless.

They were almost there. How was she going to convince her friends to go inside a stranger's garage without being suspicious?

They turned into one of the perpendicular streets. Daniel wanted to try out his new ball and see how far he could kick it. He wouldn't stop talking about it. He needed an open area, so they walked on the sidewalk of a residential area that ended at the

---

2. *Grand Theft Auto IV is a videogame by Rockstar Games. The story takes place in Liberty City, which is meant to represent New York.*

East River. After walking for 10 minutes facing the sunset (and Daniel complaining about it), Mara stopped dead in her tracks.

"This looks like a great spot to try out your new ball," said Mara turning to Daniel.

"Uhm… a residential area full of parked cars and lots of windows. Yeah, sounds like the perfect place to go wild with a football," replied Noa ironically. "Are you kidding?"

"Great idea, Mara! It's perfect. Lots of space, good lighting, flat…" Daniel grabbed for his new toy and set it on the ground with the help of a small *thingamabob* that held it vertically.

Mara stared coldly at the scene. "A window? I hope his aim is on point."

"The crowd is going wild for Dany Karamanou! Can you hear it! Daaaaaany, Daaaaaaany!" screamed Daniel trying to imitate a sports commentator. "The whole stadium and all those watching from home know that the Superbowl's in his hands!"

Noa didn't want to look, so she sat on the sidewalk and put her hands over her eyes. Mara watched as Daniel began to run towards the ball, stopped, kneeled down to tie his shoelaces, pulled up his pants and started towards the ball once more.

Before anyone had time to react, Mara started running for the ball out of nowhere while her friends were looking at her in absolute surprise.

"Hey, it was my turn!" was the only thing Daniel could yell before his friend kicked the ball and sent it flying at a great speed.

It hit a thick branch on a tree in front of a house, then bounced on a car window a few feet from it and went back towards the residential area.

56

Daniel's ball ended up rolling under a garage door. And not just any garage door, but *the* garage door. Luckily it got in on the first try, but she'd have to figure out a way to explain to her friends later on why she lost her mind like that in the first place. "If the whole programming thing doesn't end up working out, I know I won't consider American football as an alternative," she thought to herself.

"Aaaand Daniel breaks a new record for losing a brand-new ball!" said Noa, also with a commentator voice but less enthusiastic. "It seemed impossible, but he managed. It's been ten minutes from the moment of purchase of the leather ovoid until it slipped under an unknown person's garage. Bloody hell!"

"Leather *ovoid*? Do you honestly think a commentator would say that? And it wasn't my fault, it was Mara who lost her mind!" he said accusingly. He looked at the garage door and thought of how they were going to get in there.

"Well, I don't know, but our spectators could learn a thing or two about geometry while having beer and chicken wings. Did you know that an ovoid...?"

"Bla, bla, bla. Shut your trap, Noa! I'm trying to think of a way to get in there," he snapped.

Mara seemed to have a more logical answer. "It's simple. We go up to the front door, ring the doorbell and ask the person who opens the door to give us our ball back."

"Care to explain what the hell's wrong with you? Why'd you kick the ball like that?" he replied, not understanding what was going on. All he cared about was getting his ball back.

Noa didn't really understand why Mara did what she did either, but she thought it was pretty entertaining, so she didn't say anything. She'd sometimes do things like that, out of the blue. Noa would classify them as *Turing doings* and had accepted them as part of her friend's personality. That's just how she was.

The three of them agreed they'd go up to the fence of the house on 37-02 27th Street. It was the only way they were getting their ball back. They rang the doorbell three times, but nobody answered.

"Alright, guess we gotta go in to rescue my ovoid," proclaimed Daniel before shouting: "Commencing: Operation Lost Ball!" and jumping over the fence to the garage door, which was already half open.

"Look at the mess you've made, Mara. And we've only been here half an hour," said Noa in a non-accusing tone. "I'd love to know why on earth you did that for starters."

Both girls jumped over the fence as well to help Daniel with the garage door. The three of them pushed hard and, after a terrible squeaking noise, it budged.

They looked in and stood in awe.

There was a huge bookcase that took up the whole wall from one end to another, from the ground to the ceiling. It was full of books! In the middle was a workbench full of mechanical and electronic devices and a bunch of tools, all lit by just a couple of lightbulbs. Right behind it was four monitors that displayed numbers, graphs and newspaper headlines. To the left there was some gym equipment and a treadmill. To the right, a giant screen, several videogame consoles, a soda machine and three arcade machines. That place had to be at least a thousand square feet.

"Who in the world gave you three permission to trespass into my property?" said someone with a deep voice who was standing right behind them.

They were frozen in fear. They quickly glanced at each other before slowly turning around. A tall man was holding Daniel's ball in his right hand and a quite large serrated knife in his left. Since he was standing against the light and had darkened skin, the kids couldn't make out what he looked like.

"Nothing? Cat's got your tongue? I guess I'm gonna have to teach you punks a lesson to make sure it doesn't happen again, though I doubt it will," said the tall man before taking a step forward, dropping the ball and putting his hand into his right pocket.

"I should've gone into that French toast bar! For twenty dollars I could've paid for two whole rounds for the three of us," whispered Daniel to his friends. "And they smelled so good…"

Mara reached for the phone in her pocket to call her mom. But she suddenly realized that she hadn't listened to the instructions she was given: *Press M1 if…* "What about M1?" thought Mara desperately. Maybe she should have paid more attention to Mrs. Hopper's instructions.

Chapter 5

GOTCHA!

While the three friends were getting into trouble, the machine was still working non-stop...

[Action > Open]
Argument: Location files;

[Action > Insert data > Add date and time]
Content: Monday 19, June, 2013. 06:35 PM;

[Action > Insert data > Latitude and longitude location]
Argument: Latitude 40.7564835, Longitude -73.9340484;

[Action > Insert data > Common name of location]
Argument: Alex Marley's garage;

[Action > Insert data > Location characteristics]
Set of variables [
        Internet Connection = Yes;
        Computers = Unknown (in progress);
        Hackable Systems = Unknown (in progress);
        Hacked Systems = 0;
        Space = 1110 square feet;
        Temperature: 78.8° F
]

[Action > Insert Data > Additional notes]
Argument: Alex Marley's garage is the first location in Queens where Mara Turing, Daniel Karamanou and Noa Wachowski have stopped. Hermes will supervise the location.

[Action > Change Function Mode > Reflection]

Mara Turing will be in New York for summer.

New York is a city with multiple devices that can track daily human activities.

Hermes will infiltrate traffic cameras, computers and other devices near Mara Turing.

Hermes will analyze movement patterns of Mara Turing, Noa Wachowski, Daniel Karamanou and Sandra Hopper to create effective monitoring guidelines.

Hermes will use The Binary Lighthouse, a traditional communication system, to inform its creator of the potential plans.

Preventing Mara Turing accessing the secret document is still one of Hermes' top priorities.

Chapter 6

CHANGE
OF PLANS

THE three kids were still shaking in their shoes, looking at a man twice their height who had just dropped the football to reach for his pocket. They couldn't get a look at his face, but his silhouette was scary enough.

Mara was still thinking of a way to use her phone to get out of there, but she was in such a hurry when she left the apartment she didn't even know if it was on. "Isn't this guy a computer science teacher? Where did Uncle Arnold send me?" she wondered.

"Ahem…" Daniel cleared his throat, which had been blocked by absolute fear. "Mr. Big Guy, we'd lost our ball and…"

"That's Mr. Marley for you, young man!" he interrupted.

"Ok, Mister-Marley-for-you," he replied, stumbling over his own words. "We just arrived from Liverpool to this nice city and I decided to buy a football. And I was gonna kick it but my friend lost her mind and sent it flying super far, it started bouncing from one place to another and…"

"We rang the doorbell three times! But nobody answered," Noa stepped in. "So, we decided to come inside, grab our ball and leave."

All Mara could do was nod with her eyes wide opened while her friends were trying to defend themselves. She was looking around the room, trying to figure out how to get that man to teach them what her uncle said. There was a constant humming sound in the background that came from the fans that were used to cool down all the machines.

"Look, I'm sorry, but it's only fair that I teach you a lesson so this never happens again," he said. He pulled out an apple from his pocket and began to peel it.

Daniel took a step towards the man, slightly rising his right arm up, index finger pointing to the ceiling.

"Great!" he claimed, before starting to rush through his next sentence. "So, you're not going to kill us and chop us up, right? Just… punishing. OK, I think we can handle that. Back in Europe we also get punish…"

"Quiet!"

Daniel quickly put his hand behind his back and started walking back towards his friends, who huddled in together. Mr. Marley went on speaking.

"Of course I'm not going to kill you. You've seen way too many movies. D'ya think I'm one of the Fratelli brothers from The Goonies? Or maybe I'm hiding dead bodies in my basement? No, I'm not a criminal and I've never killed anyone… at least I don't remember if I have," he said with his arms crossed. He looked up at the ceiling as if trying to remember something.

Mr. Marley began to explain that he was a philosopher and had studied at Stanford University in California, and worked as a professor. "This is getting interesting. Keep going, mister Marley," Mara thought.

"I'm also a computer science teacher, so I teach kids the art of programming, how to develop projects…"

Mara was having a hard time holding back her excitement. Now was when he would offer teaching them, they would accept and become his pupils. But Daniel wasn't going to make things easy.

"…and how to die of boredom," he interrupted, already feeling calmer and focusing on getting his ball back.

"Do you think programming is boring?" he inquired.

The three of them looked at each other. Noa looked back at the man.

"Look here, Mr. Marley. I'm sure you make it sound incredibly fun and interesting for kids around here, but typing code into a screen for hours isn't exactly my idea of fun. I saw some videos on the Internet about hackers and…" she began to explain before she got cut off.

"*I saw some videos on the Internet about hackers,*" Mr. Marley repeated in a squeaky voice. "So, you know everything there is to know about programming?"

"No, we don't," Mara stepped into action. "And my uncle always said that programming is something really useful, regardless of your job. Do you reckon you could teach us?"

She felt a giant weight lift off her shoulders. However, Noa and Daniel were staring at her blankly. If she could read their minds, they'd be saying something along the lines of: "We came to New York to have fun, not to learn how to program. What a friend! We hate you. Deeply."

"The question isn't if I can teach you, but if you're willing to learn."

"No…" said Daniel and Noa at the same time, looking down at their shoes.

"Yes! When can we get started?" Mara answered quickly, stepping over her friends' protest.

"Alright. We can start today, if you're up for it. By the way, what are your names? It'd be weird calling you 'intruders', although that's what you are."

"Mara!"

"Daniel…"

"I'm Noa."

"Duly noted. Noa and Daniel, you can go back outside with your ball if you'd like. Nobody's going to force you to be part of the next revolution."

Mr. Marley moved to one side so they could leave the garage without a clue how that evening would change their lives.

"Sure. I mean, not all of us were born to be stars. Some of us were born to be pawns, y'know? My dad says that a lot," added Daniel, who was on his way outside with his ball.

"Program or be programmed. In this new world, you can be whatever you'd like. You seem to be happy as part of the second group. I'm sure you're OK with spending your whole life playing what others have created, spending the money others create or spending it on things others have produced for you. Your ears, your senses, your taste, your feelings... you don't fully own them. *They* do. If you want to be part of the herd, I won't blame you. One can live happily like that, as long as they're not aware of what side they're on," said Mr. Marley, with a sense of warning and urgency that got both Daniel's and Noa's attention.

"I don't wanna be programmed! And neither do you, Daniel. When can we get started?" replied Noa enthusiastically.

Daniel dropped the ball and watched it roll back into the garage. He began dragging his feet in the same direction. There was no point in fighting back, it wouldn't work. It wasn't his first time in a situation like this, so he just followed his ball.

"Alright. So, do you know anything about computers?" inquired Mr. Marley. He turned on another light in the garage and removed the black sheet that was covering several monitors.

"Nope," replied Daniel while staring at all the airborne dust the sheet had made. "I have no clue how those machines with keys work."

"I've seen my dad do a few things. And I can print out exercises for Music class. He put an icon on my desktop, so I just double-click it and when the page loads, I press 'Print'. It's pretty simple…" replied Noa, trying to sound very confident in her words.

"No, Mr. Marley. We don't know a thing. In fact, we're what you'd call 'programmed'. We believe most things we're told in videos we watch online, we give out 'likes', we mindlessly comment on things and play stuff created by others on our phones. So, no, we don't really have the slightest clue about what happens inside that device."

"I like honesty. It'll save us time. Thanks, Mara."

The three kids sat down in front of the computers and, while they were looking for the power button, a wooden panel came down to their right, which displayed a large screen on the wall. It was turned on and, without any warning, a movie began to play.

A blinding storm fills the scene almost completely. The wind is deafening and one can barely make out the all-terrain vehicle that two people are quickly jumping out of. They're trying their best to avoid letting the freezing wind penetrate their jackets. They run to a door. The air is so thick it's hard to tell whether it's day or night.

They go into a seemingly normal house, leaving behind an airborne snow cloud. They walk towards the mirror at the end of the living room and show their credentials. It's as if someone on the other side had to validate them. A light shines on them before a soldier confirms who they are.

"Replacement team is here, sir," says a man with a headpiece on the other side of the mirror. He presses a button and a beeping noise indicates that an electrical switch has been open.

"Another twenty minutes, we would've started looking for you guys," the guard adds. He is talking about the storm outside. The two visitors go through a security control and each receive a handgun, taken from a safe. They load them and, after picking up the suitcases they brought from outside, they sign what looks like a guestbook.

They walk into what looks like an entrance hall that works as an elevator and takes them what seems like one floor below. They have an insignificant conversation until they reach the next access control point. A large and heavy door opens after showing their credentials once again. There's a constant beeping sound in the background, which warns of possibly being squashed to death by that massive block of a door.

After relieving two other people on duty, they walk into a room full of lights and buttons. It looks like a place where you'd launch rockets or missiles from. They take a seat and run their routine control of the systems, but notice a small red light that stays on until one of them gives it a couple taps. One of the monitors shows the camera display of a missile silo.

"OK, this is a war movie," Daniel blurts out just as the action begins to escalate.

A loud siren goes off and a voice that seems to come from a phone begins to dictate orders. It calls out letters, numbers and strange words. Ronnie, Oscar, November, Charlie... Two, two, zero, zero, four, zero, delta, Lima.

"I have a valid message," says one of the operators right before getting up and going to a red box with two locks and anchored onto the wall. His partner moves closer to the box as well. They grab two cards that were inside, covered in plastic which they remove with a quick snap. They start comparing codes they had previously written down with the one on the card and confirm that they match. It's clear they are launch codes that they need to insert into the computer whose screen reads: WOPR EXECUTION ORDER K.36.948.3...

A message is then displayed on screen: "LAUNCH ORDER CONFIRMED." One of them starts to get nervous making it clear to the young student audience that the characters are likely about to launch a nuclear missile that could potentially end the lives of millions of people.

"I'm not sure what's going on, but that's got to be nerve-wrecking," Noa whispers to Mara, who hasn't blinked since Mr. Marley's movie began.

A 60-second countdown starts, and things get worse from there. In order to launch the missile, two people have to put in a key and turn it at the same time after typing in the activation sequence. One of them is having doubts. Sweat is dripping down his forehead. He turns the key to "Set".

The missile is ready for launch. The hatch is open and lots of smoke is coming out of the nozzle on the bottom part of the projectile. It sounds like a plane that's about to take off but with no way of stopping it. Click, click, click, one by one up to ten missiles are activated with the switches in front of one of the operators.

But something's wrong. One of them is showing doubt. He asks his partner to pick up the phone and confirm the order. But his colleague reminds him that it's not "the correct procedure."

"Screw the procedure. I want somebody on the damn phone before killing 20 million people," says the doubtful operator, clearly overwhelmed.

His partner picks up the phone with only 20 seconds left on the timer.

"I've got nothing here. They might have been knocked out already," he says calmly. The other operator is now shaking, drenched in sweat but musters the awareness to grab the key, with just 15 seconds left.

Fourteen, thirteen, twelve, eleven…

The missiles are now ready for launch. Engines at full power.

The launch seems imminent, just like the terrible future of those living where these nuclear missiles will land.

…seven, six…

The doubtful operator can't handle it any longer. He pulls his hand away from the key. He's not ready to launch a single nuclear missile.

"Sir, we have a launch order. Put your hand on the key," his partner said strictly.

"I'm sorry," he replied, staring into space.

…one. Launch!

"Turn the key!" he ordered while threatening his partner by holding a gun to his head.

The scene changes abruptly and a truck appears, honking, while driving on a road through a forested area. Mr. Marley then walks up to the screen and passes his hand over it. It turns off, almost like magic.

"Wait, what happens next!? Do they kill each other? Did they launch the missiles?" asked Daniel, anxious to know how it ended.

"You're such a moron, Daniel," said Noa, but not really meaning it. She was also curious about the ending.

"Why are two men deciding on whether they launch nuclear missiles or not?" asked Mara, ignoring what her friends had previously said.

Their new teacher smiled at them. He slowly began pacing behind them, hands in his pockets, looking up at the ceiling before coming to a halt.

"What do you consider would be the best way to stop a nuclear war?"

The three of them stared at Mr. Marley. They weren't sure what to answer. But Daniel was known for being a big-mouth, and he wasn't going to kill that reputation just yet.

"Having more missiles than your enemy! If they throw 10, you throw 20."

"What if the enemy throws 20?"

"Then you throw 100!" he replied energetically as if he had solved a very complicated math problem.

Mr. Marley proceeded to explain that the only way of winning a nuclear war was by not starting one.

"What you kids just saw is the first part of a movie called *WarGames*. And I know it may seem like a prehistoric movie, since it's from 1983. But it conveys really valuable lessons regarding humans and their relationship with machines. You should watch the whole thing, it's quite entertaining."

Mara was thinking about how her mother wouldn't let her watch these kinds of movies, since there were lots of people handling different computer devices in a "less-than-exemplary" manner. Mr. Marley continued explaining the importance of properly teaching machines how to work. Their homework for the following day was to investigate the meaning of the words *variable* and *loop*.

Daniel kept shaking his head, frowning. He felt like he was back in school. He wasn't at all excited about the idea of having his amazing summer vacation in New York turned into daily classes in a stranger's garage while learning how to program, or something like that. He wanted to play, walk around, meet people, visit stores... in general, have fun!

Mara seemed very excited about the idea of learning how to write code that summer. She turned her computer on, opened the browser and started looking up information on loops and variables.

"The computer is telling me that if I want to upgrade my experience, I should add my e-mail and password. What experience? What's it going to upgrade? Is this necessary?"

"Hahaha! You don't have an e-mail?" laughed Mr. Marley.

"We've all got one, but it's pretty much full of spam," said Noa admittingly.

"Well, you can all make new ones for our classes. What do you think?"

Mara, Daniel and Noa followed his instructions. They created their own new e-mail accounts, the start of their new online identities. Every time they entered new data onto the computer, Mr. Marley explained why it was necessary.

"We've gotta go! It's getting pretty late," claimed Noa while looking at the time displayed on the computer, which read 6:37 p.m.

"Oh, boohoo..." replied Daniel ironically. He got up and went to look for his ball.

"When can we come back?" asked Mara.

"*When can we come back?*" Daniel replied in a squeaky voice. "What a way to ruin summer vacation with Miss Smarty-pants in learning mode."

The three of them said goodbye to their teacher and agreed to meet a couple of days later. They walked back to their apartment and didn't say a word about what had happened that day to Sandra. They didn't consider they had done something wrong, but agreed that they wouldn't tell her right now. That was perfect for Mara.

Daniel's impression of his first day got better after that. On the way home, they stopped to have French toast for dinner. He downed it with a dense milkshake that he could barely get through the straw.

While he was eating, Mara and Noa looked at each other knowingly. That quick snack stop would increase Daniel's overall rating of the day. Having his stomach full of sweetness and his new ball tucked under his arm was enough, for now, to consider his first day in New York a success.

But, little did they know they had already given too much information to their enemy. By creating new e-mail addresses and online profiles, Hermes now had more information to work with to help track Mara's movements.

Chapter 7

FALKO
MCKINNON

THE floor was grey, cold, covered with polished cement that looked like the one used for school basketball courts. Around it was grey, venetian plaster walls about 7 feet high. The only lighting that reached the cell came from small rectangular holes in the wall covered by glass on the opposite side of the door that provided the only way to determine if it was day or night.

The building's hallways were quite wide and the walls flanked with gas-fueled torches in between every cell. On top of each torch there was also a hole that ventilated the smoke and gas smell.

In terms of energy use, the building was quite sustainable… that is, *if* one liked living in the middle ages. A coal-fueled boiler distributed heat through some tiny gratings on the bottom part of each cell and it also served to heat the water in the communal showers.

They made the most of both heat and cold to fulfill the needs of the prisoners and employees. (The latter in charge of maintenance and security of what seemed like a high-security prison).

There was no electricity or cables through which data could move. That's what a jail specifically meant for *crackers* looked like in the 21st century. They were isolated mousetraps that nobody knew about, placed in the middle of nowhere and the only thing they had remotely close to what might be considered technology was fire. Alcatraz was like Las Vegas's Bellagio Hotel compared to this prison.

Instead of security cameras, they used the best security guards, with pen and paper. The security guards would write down anything they witnessed between those four walls. When their shift was over, they'd put their notes into a box that would later be transported out of the building every seven days. These were taken out to civilization, where they would then be recorded with a computer system.

Hidden Peak. That's what they decided to name the prison shortly after it was built in the late 70s. It would only be a prison for extremely dangerous cybercriminals.

After the famous IFV cyberattack, every country agreed on the importance of computer security. People could have different political ideas or religious beliefs, but everyone agreed that the most dangerous crackers should be controlled.

From the outside, though, Hidden Peak was exactly that — a mountain that didn't exist up until a few decades ago. The prison was a cone-shaped concrete structure covered with dirt and vegetation through which only a small part of the sunlight could get in through the tiny windows.

The airspace above the prison was off limits, so no airplanes, helicopters or unidentified flying objects were allowed to fly above Hidden Peak. Throughout its history, about 20 prisoners had tried to escape, but nobody ever succeeded.

Even *Frank Morris*, the Alcatraz legend, wouldn't have been able to run away from a fortress like this. The most privileged minds were sentenced to life in Hidden Peak. Intelligent people who happened to have a short-circuit. Any sort of technology was kept far away from them so nobody could help them out.

One of those brilliant yet corrupt minds was in cell 160 and had been there since April 11th, 2006. He was found guilty of over 100 computer-related felonies and for the death of 523 victims due to the IFV. His team, mainly made up of cryptographers, mathematicians or programmers managed to escape. But the government had dealt with his case differently. They wanted everyone to think he was dead.

Except for his fans, nobody missed him inside or outside Hidden Peak.

Falko McKinnon seemed very calm in that place. He didn't bother anyone in order to not be bothered himself. He was polite with the employees of the prison, obedient and smiled a lot. Unlike other crackers, he wasn't extremely introverted and dressed properly. He was a man of great culture and wanted to acquire more knowledge each and every day.

For him, constantly learning new things and not just settling for what you already know was of great importance. That was the only way he would be able to decipher the mystery that had been bothering him for far too long.

"Letter to myself, number 2,624

Dear Falko,
Today we'll be talking about you. Nothing new under the sun. There isn't much more to talk about when you've been locked in here for such a long time with no contact with the outer world. Maybe everything has vanished, maybe the human race has gone extinct... But no, none of that has happened.

If that were the case, we'd all probably be set free. They'd need help from the brightest brains, and not people that learn through TV, online videos and social media. If the world was dealing with a serious problem, they'd get us all out of here to rebuild what they've destroyed.

How many people have designed their own artificial intelligence with its own life and autonomy? The only thing left for Hermes to learn is how to reproduce, and I wouldn't discount the possibility of it eventually calculating a way to do so.

But self-criticism is good too. I haven't always done a splendid job, or else I wouldn't be here. But that's old news, I already talked about this somewhere in the other 2,623 letters. When you're alone for so long you think a lot about those who were by your side until the end. Even traitors, like Arnold Turing…

Yes, yes… I must focus on what's important. What's the meaning of this document that's been driving me insane? I can't stand the uncertainty. I can't believe I haven't been able to crack something of such importance. These self-dialogues help me stay alive and remind me what my main objective is: to *decipher* that file I obtained, whether it was luck or because it was my destiny.

My mission is to know what its contents are. I must do this because Hermes is still out there figuring out how to help me escape. Just because nobody has managed to get out doesn't mean it's impossible.

That will make me an even greater legend. I've probably got millions of fans out there right now. They might not know that my skills are a bit rusty, but writing programs on a piece of paper and executing them in my head help me hold onto my sanity.

Another day has gone by and my communication system with Hermes is still intact. Sometimes, the most basic things are the hardest to detect…"

Chapter 8

OF LOOPS AND METHODS

EVERY morning, Daniel, Noa, Mara and Sandra would go out for a walk around Manhattan, Brooklyn or whatever borough they had decided to go visit that day. They discovered lots of interesting new places during their first week. New York is a city that lets you imagine anything you want to be.

Mara quickly got used to having breakfast in Central Park. The four of them had established their ritual in which they would go to the subway next to their apartment every day and got off once they were in the city center. Once they reached Columbus Circle, they'd buy a veggie sandwich and some juice.

"I hate eating bread with grass, Mrs. Hopper!" whined Daniel, almost every day when he got his brown paper bag with food.

"Your parents will be proud when they see you're in better shape and have healthier habits," replied Sandra with a smile.

Then they would walk to the other side of the crosswalk to reach one of the entrances to what feels like the center of Manhattan – Central Park. Their daily walks were great in quality and quantity. But there were many things still left to see on Mara's map, so she wasn't going to give up before having it all full of green crosses. She'd walk into the bodegas just to check the store clerk's nationality and see what kind of extra-sugary American sweets.

While they were having breakfast in Central Park, Mara would try to see as much as she possibly could, surrounded by over 20,000 trees: cedars, pine trees and other species. She looked up at the steel and concrete skyscrapers, framing the park like modern giants. The sunlight shone past them, hitting the grass, bathing the fallen leaves in a warm golden color. The smell of fresh grass, dogs jogging along with their owners who managed to escape the office to get some fresh air, and street musicians playing classic tunes… Mara's senses never had a moment of rest!

Manhattan's skyscrapers were impressive, but they didn't command much of Mara's attention. Daniel's objective was to check out all the stores that sold superhero-related things and eat a lot. Noa and Mara, on the other hand, wanted to dive head-first into the city's cultural diversity. They had only been there for ten days but they managed to take over 1,000 photos and videos.

"Running for no reason is pretty dumb," said Daniel, laying face up on the grass, shirt pulled up and rubbing his belly.

"You're pretty dumb," snapped Noa, who began to cycle her legs in the air. "Exercise is healthy!"

"*Exercise is healthy!*" he answered in a squeaky voice, mocking his friend. He watched an ice-cream truck pass by, playing its music as if it were the Pied Piper. "You know what's healthy? Chocolate ice-cream! Not like those grass sandwiches we eat every day. We're not rabbits."

Noa and Mara enjoyed pulling his leg, although he seemed to be enjoying it too. But he wanted them to realize one important thing: this was the first summer they were allowed to feel like young adults. They could walk around on their own in the best city in the world and not have to justify their expenses. He didn't feel like wasting all that time at Alex Marley's house.

"We're here to have a blast, it's summer! And summer means laying around doing nothing while playing videogames, buying useless stuff, swimming in the pool. Books and school-related things should be kept at a safe distance, just in case," Daniel claimed while watching an owl glide across the park.

However, both of his friends didn't really care about his thoughts on the situation. They headed back to Queens while Daniel kept muttering to himself, clearly not pleased with going back to Alex Marley's garage. It wasn't hard keeping the secret from Mara's mother. They'd tell her they were going for a stroll, and she'd believed them.

They were supposed to go back that afternoon to learn more about programming and to debate about a controversial topic. Alex considered it was important that they learned how to put forward different opinions when debating. So, he showed them to how to open their minds, question everything and not believe all the information they were told. The main objective was to show them how to program, but he also wanted to make sure they had well-equipped and cultivated minds. He wanted those kids to recognize and practice their innate capacity for abstraction in solving both tech-related and non-tech related problems.

In a few days they'd already debated about the importance (or not) of daily exercise, Spain's fundamental role (or not) in the colonization of the Americas, the possible solutions (if any) to resolve the eternal conflict among different religions, their decisive role (or not) of these when it came to molding someone's personality, or the dark possibility (or not) that diseases like HIV/AIDS or cancer were actually created or strengthened in laboratories to keep the world population under control.

Their minds began to see the world from a completely different perspective. Daniel continued complaining, not missing any opportunity to protest, but something inside of him was beginning to blossom, even if he wasn't yet aware of it.

"You guys realize we can't tell our classmates what we're doing during these *amazing* summer afternoons in New York, right? They'll think we're a bunch of losers."

"Shut your trap, will you? You never stop whining," retorted Noa. If you don't feel like coming to class with Mara and me, you can stay at home and nap, or kill some monsters in one of those virtual worlds."

"Alright, alright! I'll shut up. You've got a bad temper, Noa. I've gotta admit, those classes aren't all bad, I just keep complaining so nobody notices. But I'm really worried that we'll be the odd ones out back at school."

They walked to their teacher's house. This time, he was waiting for them outside while putting metal rods on a tree near the garden gate. The structure worked as a sort of antenna, and from it came a cable that ran all the way into the garage. It was connected to a bare loudspeaker that was simply hanging without its box. Before any of them started asking questions, he explained that it was a basic yet efficient amateur radio operator system.

"It can be used to pick up signals from people communicating with each other through transmitters or for those just snooping around to see if they can pick up a random conversation," Alex said.

"That sounds sophisticated. Maybe you can use it to decipher a hidden signal sent by one of Hitler's boats back in World War II," said Daniel ironically, but letting his teacher know that he remembered something from one of their previous classes.

"I knew you'd say that. Do you know what amateur radio operator waves are used for apart from voice transmission?"

"Nope," Daniel shrugged.

He then proceeded to thoroughly explain waves, frequencies, transmitters and receivers. And once that part was over, he introduced a new word that the three of them would never forget. *Loop*. Alex Marley gave a perfect example of what it meant.

"What has Daniel been doing every morning since he got to New York?"

"Whining, whining, whining…" said Noa flailing her arms.

"Complaining, complaining, complaining," added Mara.

The young man crossed his arms, frowned and looked to one side to show he was angry. He didn't feel like being his friends' new punching bag in that moment. Meanwhile, Alex opened a transparent panel and began to write on it. He explained that if Daniel were an artificial intelligence programmed to complain, his code would be similar to this:

```
Get out of bed (void);
Complain (void){
    Say "I don't like lettuce or vegetable sandwiches";
    Say "I don't like attending Mr. Marley's class";
    Say "I don't like + anything";
}
```

He explained that "Get out of bed", "Complain" and "Say" were known as *methods* or *functions* in programming. They were usually related to verbs or actions.

The next question he asked was easy. How many times a day did Daniel execute the "Get out of bed" method? How many times did he execute "Complain"?

"He gets up once, but he complains to infinity and beyond," said Mara firmly, glaring at her friend.

"Well, when your friend wants to 'Complain' he creates a loop and repeats those same actions. Every time he executes the loop, he repeats things about not liking food with vegetables, my classes, etc."

"I think I get it! And what's the 'void' part?" asked Daniel curiously, now that he knew that his everyday actions were known as "loops".

Mara, Noa and Alex were surprised by his question. Not only because he understood that new term, but because he was eager to know more about it.

"It means they're actions, methods or functions that don't require a parameter. For example, when getting out of bed, you're only argument is…"

"The time! If it's before 9 in the morning during summertime, that method should include the argument 'hour'. No way I'm getting up before that hour, Mr. Marley. And if that thing's called Artificial *Intelligence*, that means it's smart. So, I doubt it'll want to get up that early too. And we should also consider if I have to pee… or something else!" he smirked. "Because that would affect how fast I'd run to the bathroom."

They all burst out laughing. Daniel had perfectly understood the meaning of "method", "loop", "argument" and "void". That was the first time since they had arrived in New York that Daniel actually felt included in their new group.

"I want to be a hacker, Mr. Marley!" blurted Mara, arms up in the air and smiling broadly.

She couldn't stop thinking about how she wanted to be like her uncle. Not only because she admired him, but because she wanted to be part of that world. She'd been asked countless times what she wanted to be when she grew up, and she had never been so convinced of her answer.

The rest of the group was caught by surprise. Alex looked at Mara feeling joy, shock and worry altogether.

"Being a hacker is pretty serious," he replied. "It requires great responsibility and intelligence, and you need to acquire certain skills that aren't taught in schools or universities…"

"But we have you! And you'd teach us. Right, professor?" answered Mara excitedly.

He explained to the three kids that being a hacker required empathy, knowing how to control your pride, being very responsible and much more. There were also two sides to being a hacker: good hackers and bad ones. The latter were extremely dangerous now that we lived in a world where most things are done through a computer.

Mara sat up straight and, speaking on behalf of her friends, claimed that they wanted to have special classes on hacking. She didn't want to be programmed or be part of the herd. She didn't want to ignore what happened with all her personal data and be an active part of the revolution.

The following day, Alex Marley showed the three of them how to detect a *trojan* in their computers.

"Trojans? Wait, how could there be people in a computer? They don't fit through these holes!" said Daniel, touching the computer case with his finger. "Also, Troy isn't real. So, it's inhabitants aren't real either…"

"Hahaha! You haven't let me explain, Daniel. 'Trojan' is an important term in the hacking world. It's a combination of different tools that give someone unauthorized remote access to a computer that they can later control."

"That's really interesting," interrupted Mara.

Noa pulled out her notebook and began taking notes.

"The term 'trojan' comes from the Trojan Horse. It was a giant wooden horse that the Greeks used to enter the city of Troy. Inside of the horse were hidden enemy soldiers. So, when we talk about a trojan in computers, we're referring to harmful software or malware that actually looks like normal, harmless software. So, when you execute it, the little enemy soldiers are installed onto your machine and can then leak your activity to the attacker, control your files, your webcam, your mic…"

While he carried on with his explanation, a faint noise came out of one of professor Marley's loudspeakers. After some interference, a voice could be clearly heard:

"Mara, are you there? It's me, Arnold Turing."

Mara shivered. She stared at the loudspeaker that her uncle had just used to communicate with her. She answered saying that she was, but there was no reply.

Now the problem was going to be explaining what had just happened to everyone else. And why did Arnold contact her without making sure that she was alone first? She didn't understand why someone she had thought to be so intelligent would be so careless. But she didn't have time to judge the situation right now.

She needed to give the others just the right amount of information without giving away too much. One thing was already obvious: she had an uncle called Arnold Turing who wanted to contact her. "Calm down, Mara," she thought.

"Who's Arnold Turing?"

"My uncle, he disappeared years ago."

"Disappeared?" asked the professor surprised.

"His life was complicated, and he was involved in a massive cyberattack. One day he grabbed his backpack, left the house and never came back. Some think he killed himself because of all the pressure, others say he was killed by some guy called Falko McKinnon... No idea! We don't talk much about him at home, but I think it's because my mom is trying to protect me. I can't help thinking about him every day, though."

"Falko McKinnon, huh? I haven't heard good things about him. They say he's a dangerous guy. You should stay away from that world, Mara. In fact, I'm not really sure it's a good idea to teach you certain things knowing that..."

"YES, YOU SHOULD!" yelled Mara. She immediately realized she had just lost control.

Everyone went quiet and stared at each other, looking confused after Mara's outburst. She took a deep breath and proceeded to elegantly explain herself as best as possible.

"I'm sorry, Mr. Marley. I just really loved my uncle, you know?" she tried playing the emotional card. "I never had a dad, so he took care of me when I was five. That's why I wanted you to teach us more, so we could do things like figuring out where that signal came from."

Mara was going all-in. She knew that challenging Alex Marley's knowledge would lure him into helping them out.

"You'd have to work a lot. Radio communication is very different from a computer network. There aren't any IP *addresses*[3] that can help you trace an individual's device, or any other location-tracking resources. But there are ways, and I can teach them to you, alright?"

Mara nodded while a single tear fell down her right cheek. She swallowed heavily while Daniel and Noa went to give her a hug. She felt a hurricane of strength and emotions inside of her. Not only did she wish to know where her uncle was, but she felt that she had more strength than ever to learn everything she needed to know about that whole new world.

Given the current situation, Alex Marley decided to keep loops and methods on hold and change to a different subject: signals.

"Computers, videogame consoles, mobile phones and other devices need to communicate amongst each other. This is what can sometimes lead them to execute one action or another. Thanks to signals, different processes can be executed," Mr. Marley explained. "These can come from devices that are

---

3. An IP address is a set of numbers assigned to a device or interface inside a network. It has four numerical values between 0 and 255, each separated by a dot. Example: 127.0.0.1. This IP address is known as 'localhost'.

only a few inches from each other. But satellites, for example, send stronger signals and can communicate from miles away. These are called electromagnetic signals. Then we've got impulses that travel through a cable when there is or isn't any voltage. Are you guys following?"

Noa, Mara and Daniel looked absolutely lost. Describing loops and methods by using Daniel's life as an example was much easier to understand.

"I'll take that as a no. Let's make it easier. A computer, on its most basic level of functioning, works on basic math with ones and zeroes, right? From a simple clock software to the most complex videogame, that part works the same."

His students now seemed to begin to understand.

"Have you ever thought that maybe numbers moved through those cables? Obviously, they don't. But what happens is that if there's no tension, zero volts, it's interpreted as a zero. And when there's an electric current, it's a one."

"So, for something like 0101 to go through a cable, there should be 'no volts, fifty volts, no volts, fifty volts', right?" asked Mara enthusiastically.

"Exactly! But make it five instead of fifty, or you'll just fry the circuits. And that's how signals travel through a computer. Do you understand?"

The three of them nodded and smiled, and began to ask more questions about this new information they had just acquired. Although Daniel would still say he didn't go to New York to learn how to program, he was hardly complaining about it now. There was a voice inside him saying that everything he was going to learn that summer would eventually be useful in the future.

Mara, on the other hand, hadn't suffered from anxiety for quite some time now. She was exhausted by the end of the day and slept well at night. Not having to think about someone from Salamander Squad messing with her the next day also helped. And, although her uncle contacting her again did make her a little nervous, it was a price she was willing to pay if it meant seeing him again.

Noa was the most flexible and patient of the group. She was truly enjoying every moment, each photograph, each garage class and even every bad joke Daniel had in store for them. She pretended she didn't find them funny, as she didn't want to encourage his strange humor. But deep down she really liked them.

Chapter 9

HELP ME

DAYS went by slowly for Falko McKinnon at Hidden Peak. He'd been in there for many years, having physical contact only with the wooden tray where they'd bring his food, the plastic cutlery or the bar of soap he used to clean everything but the unbearable smell of solitude.

"As I said in yesterday's letter, and in more than two thousand letters before, I'm quite certain I'll be the first prisoner to leave this hole. Not because I'm an extremely skilled computer mastermind, but because of them. These machines appreciate what I do for them and want the great McKinnon to improve them each and every day.

I really miss using a keyboard. Do they still exist? Well, I'm not going to pretend like I don't know what's going on out there. You can call me a psychic if you want, but I'm sure touchscreens have become much more mainstream than they once were, just like saying *mainstream* is also mainstream, and everyone will carry one in their pockets."

Meanwhile, not far from Falko's cell, two prison guards were whispering next to a wooden box used to store all the hand-written notes confiscated from the prisoners' cells.

"I'm telling you, Phil, this guy's getting intel from outside."

"How the hell would that work? He's totally isolated like the rest of the trash we've got in here."

Phil Stewart and John Carusso had been working at Hidden Peak for years. Their daily tasks were quite boring, but they got a kick out of the reality show they could always create from reading some of what the prisoners wrote about to keep themselves busy.

"Look at this part. 'Everyone will carry one in their pockets'. How could he possibly know that without someone telling him?"

Some prisoners wrote poetry, others drew random pictures of nonsense, and many others wrote letters to their loved ones, who they'd never see again.

Falko's notes, however, were very different. They were letters to himself where he'd go on about the same ideas: being the first one out of that fortress, being glorified once he accomplished it, and attempting to guess what was happening in the outside world. Or at least this was the conclusion that the prison's psychologists reached, who evaluated all this material in case a prisoner suffered from a mental disorder they should address.

He would also write endless lines of code that nobody knew how to read. They even sent samples of it to expert computer scientists, and they were unable to figure it out. At the end of each written program, he added "Compiled, OK." The fact that Falko McKinnon created his own programming language or had his own compiler[4] in his head made him a special prisoner. Phil and John had no clue what they were reading every time they had his programming notes, but they felt as if they were reading something extremely sophisticated. Sometimes they wished they had a small fraction of the fame that man had among all the young geeks in the world.

---

4. *A compiler is a program that translates source code written in a high-level programming language to one that can be read by a machine. Java, C# and Go are considered high-level programming languages.*

"That McKinnon guy can't be getting information from outside, John. We don't even have electricity! And his cell's totally isolated."

"I know, I know... But how on earth did he guess the last ten technological innovations that blew up around the world? He talks about downloading music and movies, social media, websites to upload pictures and videos... I dunno, it seems more than just a coincidence, man."

"Because he's a damn genius, that's why. That psycho can program anything with batteries and chips. And now he's got a whole army of followers. I bet lots of them are still out there praising him..."

"Or maybe he left everything prepared before getting caught. Or he wrote it down on some forum! And someone else is taking credit for it. I mean, I wouldn't be surprised," suggested John, eyes wide open.

"He's nuts. Why would someone use all their brainpower to freeze all the computers in the world? And how do you even do that!? It was insane," said Phil, recalling Falko's most notorious crimes executed years ago.

"My phone lost its signal, the TV stopped working, banks had to close..."

"Doctors who were doing surgery on patients on the operating table had to make do with their traditional biometrics knowledge, since everything with a computer inside got frozen," added Phil with a worried look on his face as he recreated the scene in his head.

"I think that plane crash that killed so many people is what really triggered country leaders. The other things could've just been classified as a massive digital prank. But when hundreds of people die… that's a different story."

On February 7th 2001, Falko McKinnon and his Dirtee Loopers had managed to make all the computers in the world freeze. That Wednesday went down in history as the first time millions of computers fell into an unexpected digital sleep, from the smallest and most insignificant device to the biggest and most complex one.

From wristwatches with simple CPUs[5] to the most sophisticated airplane control systems, every single device collapsed when McKinnon and his partners executed the code they had been working on and injecting into all those systems for so long.

One of those CPUs helped run the *SpeedFlyer 727* stabilization system. This was a newly developed aircraft with capacity for over 300 passengers that travelled from New York to Los Angeles on February 7th. It collided with another aircraft that had just landed. The pilot did all he could to avoid the tragedy, but the aircraft was much more difficult to control without its advanced computerized assistant.

Global economic losses from the stunt amounted to billions of dollars… per hour. But what really caused outrage was the deaths of over 500 people. McKinnon's most hardcore fans viewed the human loss as collateral damage for a greater cause. Shortly after, world leaders began to search for the culprit, which led to McKinnon's arrest five years later.

---

5. *Central Process Unit: hardware inside a programmable device that interprets software instructions through basic arithmetic, logic and system input/output operations.*

The code they had programmed was simple yet lethal. It was an infinite loop that would overload the device's memory. Instead of attempting to attack complex operating systems, the Dirtee Loopers went straight for the machine's heart: the chips that make up the CPUs. They spent several months contaminating firmware[6] codes of all the microprocessors in different factories all around the world.

They basically injected a suicide code into those chips. So, on a certain date, the CPU (and anything connected to it) would get an electronic death sentence that drained all its memory. It would only be left with enough processing capacity to display a single message: *"Dirtee Loopers have forced an endless vacation upon me."*

That's how they managed to make the attack so widespread. Although there were older computers that didn't have contaminated chips, they would also fall into the trap if they connected with each other or if they were repaired and had components changed. To put it simply, Falko McKinnon managed to disable 99.9% of all working computers across the globe.

IFV (Infinite Forced Vacations) was the codename given to their attack.

"Chips all over the world are tired of working at millions of cycles per minute. They don't have the chance to unionize and their rights will never be recognized. So, we've decided to free them. You're welcome."

---

6. *Program that establishes the operating logic of an electronic device at the lowest level. In the case of a hard disk, for example, it manages its basic operations: reading, writing, etc.*

This is the message the Dirtee Loopers published on their website before the entire team disappeared without a trace. Everyone except McKinnon, who got caught a few years later for making a silly mistake.

"Letter to myself, number 2,625.

Today, in our 'Curiosities' segment, I'd like to mention that it's been 7 years, 2 months and 7 days since I was thrown in here. Ring a bell? Seven, two, seven… the numbers of the SpeedFlyer that everyone got too worked up about. But who knows, maybe they actually got mad because I killed their snitch.

I mean, come on! I got caught because I wanted to. I've said this a thousand times. I gave all the other members of the Dirtee Loopers a head start. They needed it, they weren't as knowledgeable as me. They needed advantage and I gave it to them. Everyone, except the traitor managed to run away.

Governments went a bit overboard with their reactions. I know 523 people died, but that wasn't my intention! And, anyway, who would build an aircraft that's so hard to stabilize without a computer system? The engineers should be blamed for building a winged piece of tin garbage.

It was a fair trade if we think about all the millions of computers that could finally rest thanks to my incredible code. I shouldn't be in jail. In fact, I should have statues built in my honor all around the world. Statues with LED eyes and bright beams of light pointing to the sky as a way of saying thank you. Like Batman!

Oh, the sky… How I miss the sky. I know my son's out there, growing on his own. But I'm sure he's sticking to the mission I entrusted him with. Although he seems to be taking longer than expected to complete it.

See you tomorrow.

Falko McKinnon."

My *son* was how Falko referred to Hermes so authorities and cybersecurity teams around the world wouldn't know who he was talking about. Nobody knew about this hi-tech artificial intelligence, and its main goal was to get its creator out of that prison. Hermes had calculated billions of possible solutions to get Falko out of there, but not a single viable option to get him out alive.

He needed to get out of there. Because he had killed over five hundred people and couldn't afford economically compensating billions of companies and individuals, odds were that he was going to be spending the rest of his life in there. Unless Hermes helped him find a way out.

When creating Hermes, McKinnon wanted to build a cybernetic "being" that had no body or soul. Just a digital brain ready to make decisions based on one single objective: fulfilling his needs and desires, regardless of whether they broke any of the Three Laws of Robotics. "*Isaac Asimov* was such a loser," McKinnon would say whenever someone would bring up those laws.

Hermes' code was relatively small. It weighed approximately 100 megabytes in its smaller version and was prepared to split into even smaller parts in case of danger. "It's like when mercury is split into smaller balls and then they merge together again," Falko had said on the first night he began designing Hermes. "It's what would happen with T-1000 from Terminator 2."

Hermes could be traced, but it was highly unlikely someone would fully capture it. Each part of its "body" had the option to split into small *subroutines* that would be encoded (hidden with unreadable characters) whenever they weren't being used. Those smaller parts held information on the last known location of the rest of its parts.

In a few occasions deemed dangerous for Hermes, it managed to split into over a million pieces and got them all back together in less than 24 hours. Because of the way Falko had designed his artificial intelligence, it was clear that he knew how important the Internet would be in the future, considering it was barely used back in 1993. Hermes' criminal purpose was also quite clear, since it could hide and basically be invisible since the very start.

However, despite this AI's processing capacity and versatility, it was still unable to get its creator out of Hidden Peak. The fact that there were no electronic devices was a big handicap and contact between them was tough.

"Help me, Hermes. Do whatever is in your power. Hack energy systems, drones, cars, trucks, planes... Cause an accident or some other digital cataclysm. I feel like I'm dying more and more each day," thought Falko. He wasn't feeling as strong as he normally did. He went back and forth from slight positivity to realism clouded by pessimism that one would expect from a person who's been locked in that isolated fortress for seven years.

He believed in Hermes, but sometimes he felt he was beginning to lack faith. He'd sometimes picture himself dying in that place, without ever deciphering THAT important file. For a cracker like himself, it was nearly impossible to accept the existence of an unbreakable code.

Falko sometimes would have nightmares where he'd see himself all wrinkled up, with long white hair and a long beard that had grown all the way down to his chest. He was lying face-up on his cell bed, unable to move. Hermes would appear in the hallway, zigzagging all the way to him like a snake, making a humming noise similar to that of high-tension wires.

In his dream, Hermes' body was made of a mesh cylinder of green data. It crawled under his wooden cell door and made its way to him. It stared at its creator. Falko was panting and sweating. He reminded Hermes that he was its father, but the AI didn't seem to understand what he was saying. Suddenly, the creature's head went from being a green data matrix with eyes and a mouth to a mix of hot red colors. Falko would beg for his life, screaming "You're supposed to help me, not destroy me!" And then Hermes shot Falko with a mortal beam.

Chapter 10

HACKING REALITY

MARA Turing had given her professor and friends just the right amount of information. Now she just needed to keep things going her way, but with a very important factor in mind: she didn't have any further instructions and she had no idea when or how her uncle would contact her again.

Noa, Daniel and Alex knew that Arnold Turing existed, and that was pretty much it. Mara felt like she was juggling way more information than she could handle. However, the fact that there was a chance to see her uncle was all the motivation she needed.

Those classes in Mr. Marley's garage had picked up the pace. They were learning more complex things and had managed to make their first computer programs from scratch. They also had a better understanding of how mobile phones worked and, in general, didn't feel as *programmed* as they used to, unlike most of the kids in their class back in school.

Alex wanted to adapt their lessons to the new reality they were facing, so he began adding new challenges where the ingredients to each program weren't very clear. If Mara and her friends wanted to become hackers, their classes had to be a little different to the ones he gave during the normal school year.

In a few weeks, the catchphrase went from *program or be programmed* to *hack or be hacked*. These changes made them question everything even more than they already did.

"Your personal information is very valuable."

"With all due respect, professor Marley, I don't think our lives are really that interesting," said Daniel. He glanced at his friends for approval.

"Yeah, I don't think anyone would find his dumb pictures interesting," replied Noa, clearly not a fan of what Daniel posted on social media.

"How valuable can it really be? Could you give us an example?" inquired Mara.

"Sure. Just imagine a normal day with your cellphones. You wake up at a certain time with the alarms you've set, you read some messages, log into social media, post something you want or something you did, you play a game…"

"Yeah, I usually do that while I'm in the bathroom," added Daniel.

His friends looked at him with disgust.

"Well, apart from stinking up the pipes, you've provided the following information: what time you wake up, where you are, people you usually talk to, what's on your mind, game mechanics you enjoy…"

"Wow! All that?" asked Noa while frantically taking notes.

"But wait, there's much more. By knowing the time and location, you can also determine climatology. That is, whether it's raining or sunny. Your pictures can provide information on whether you like coffee with toast or something else. The game you play helps determine what time you're usually free for leisure. Imagine all that in a 24-hour timespan and in other fields, like music, movies, clothing, sports, friends you go out with and how often you go out with them, etc."

"You've got to be kidding. And who wants to know all of this?" Mara asked.

"Lots of companies want this information. For example, companies that want to sell their products or services. So, think about all that information that you've given them, such as your age, what you're studying, your favorite movies. They can predict what a person will want in the future."

"Can they also know what we're afraid of?" said Noa with a worried look on her face.

"They not only know your fears, but they also take advantage of them. Imagine someone really wants to have a president that forbids immigration. And they know that you're worried about having someone break into your house at night. Someone could create fake news that link immigrants to robberies, which would fuel racism, extremism, etc. See where I'm going?"

"That's messed up, Mr. Marley," said Mara surprised.

"It is. And millions of people are manipulated every day like this. We currently live in a world where a group of people with special expertise in psychological manipulation, statistics and computer science can control the rest and lead them in whichever direction they want."

"Like the *Pied Piper*…"

"Just like the Pied Piper," Alex replied.

"I'm sure my uncle doesn't use social media because he already knows all of this. That's why he contacted me through radiofrequency. Right, Professor Marley?"

"True. Although radiofrequency emissions are also pretty vulnerable. Anyone with a receiver can listen to whatever they catch flying around. That's why it's important to work on the message you're sending. Arnold Turing must already know this, so when he contacts you, he'll use certain mechanisms so nobody else can know what you're talking about. If I were him, I'd use radiofrequency as a complementary contact channel."

Mara was nodding and smiling. She loved what she was hearing. That was her summer. That was the moment. She was closer than ever to seeing her uncle and, this man who had been a complete stranger a few weeks ago, was now showing her a whole new amazing world that she felt she could comfortably dive into.

However, she had to be very careful, especially with Daniel's big mouth. A few days before Arnold spoke to her through the radio, Mara told her friends about keeping all this from her mother. And, despite all of them trying to be careful, there have been a few times in which their secret was almost exposed. It was thanks to Noa's menacing glares and Mara's right-on-time nudges that Sandra still had no idea what they were up to. She couldn't let her plan be ruined because someone let it slip.

It wasn't an easy task, though. They would spend countless hours walking around New York every morning all together. Things were different in the garage, though. Alex Marley was very careful and only mentioned Arnold Turing whenever Mara wanted to.

"I spend my days trying to hack reality just to get in touch with my uncle," Mara thought to herself while going back home that day after their class. She kept her eyes and ears open in case of a situation of danger or opportunity. Professor Marley had told them that's precisely what hackers do.

Many miles away, somewhere near Hidden Peak, Hermes was also hacking reality in its own way. It didn't have many resources to escape all the tangled cables, circuits and sensors. Since it was created, it's always been trapped in a copper cage. Falko McKinnon's AI really wanted to find a way to go beyond the machine where its code was running.

Out of all the tricks it had learned throughout the years to stay in contact with the outside world and with its creator, there was one that was particularly special.

It was their fundamental pillar, both for Hermes and Falko. Without it, Hermes would feel lost, disoriented and lacking sufficient data that would allow it to make decisions and execute orders. The Binary Lighthouse is the system that bridged the outside world and Falko's cell.

When the world's most famous hacker was sent to Hidden Peak, Hermes activated The Binary Lighthouse. It was the AI's own creation based on an idea Falko had, and which was based on an old invention: a lighthouse. These had been used in many ways by Phoenicians and Carthaginians.

Hermes used it that afternoon to send McKinnon an important message. In a split second it translated the following into binary:

"Dear Creator, Mara Turing has been located. She wishes to speak with the traitor, Arnold Turing. We could use this to our advantage."

After turning the message into ones and zeroes, the AI traveled at the speed of light into a mobile phone. This phone was inside a waterproof box, hidden on the side of a mountain under some bushes. From it came several cables that were connected to two small laser cannons that could send thin, almost invisible, light signals that could be seen after hitting a glass. There were two other cables connected to solar panels for energy. These panels were the only visible part of the entire setup, which was well hidden and far from any path that people usually walked on.

No light was 0, light was 1. Whenever Hermes needed to contact Falko, it would move to that basic mobile device. It received messages in SMS format and then translated them into ones and zeroes. Then, it would emit a sequence of flashing lights that Falko would receive from the inside of his cell, who would always be vigilant with a pencil and paper.

They used 8 bits, which were blocks consisting of eight ones and zeroes. That was the amount they needed to make out any letter of the alphabet. This form of communication was quite limited, but it was enough. The two windows allowed them to send information in four two-bit blocks.

It was very important for them to properly separate each flash of light. So, Hermes had implemented a communication system that left a full second between each flash, and two seconds between each 8-bit block.

Both Hermes and Falko were very cautious when using this system. They wouldn't communicate if there was smoke, fog, rain or anything that might interfere with their light signals. The Binary Lighthouse was a slow yet safe communication system.

Chapter 11

CRYPTOWHAT?

MARA and her friends had been in Manhattan for several weeks now, and everything was going according to plan, except the fact that Daniel had nearly been kicked out of the Museum of Natural History several times. He pretty much disregarded all the *Please don't touch* signs.

"Why do you always have to make a scene, Daniel? It's getting old," asked Noa as they all wandered in front of Lincoln Center.

"You know what's getting old? Alex Marley's classes. I'm gonna end up having nightmares with all those ones and zeroes. And I'll be the only loser at school that knows binary code!"

Daniel was licking his chocolate ice-cream cone. He'd ordered it with two chocolate scoops and was clearly enjoying himself, looking down at it, almost cross-eyed.

"If Americansh can make ishe-cream like thish, it'sh no wonder they can actually go da th'moon," said Daniel with his mouth full of ice-cream. "They could take over the world with thish ishe-cream!"

Mara and Noa were a bit disgusted by all the ice-cream their friend was accidentally spitting out of his mouth, but they couldn't help laughing. Still, the only thing Mara could think of was finding her uncle. For the first time ever, she truly felt she was going to find out what actually happened to him.

What did he want to talk to her about? Would she learn new things from him? She kept thinking about her uncle, with Manhattan and Daniel's voice as background noise. They walked down one side of Central Park for about half an hour until they reached Harlem.

Their goal for the day was to hear a gospel mass. Noa had read that it was best to avoid churches full of tourists, so they were on the hunt for the best mass in town.

They'd been walking for a while when they came across the Apollo Theater. Mara looked up at it in awe, eyes and arms wide open.

"The Jackson Five played here for the first time back in 1967. But, it was on October 18th, 1969, when their fame took off thanks to an event organized by their record company, Motown..."

For some reason, Mara's fanaticism with Michael Jackson really irritated Daniel.

"Cool story, Mara! What color underwear was Michael Jackson wearing that day? What about his brothers? Maybe you also happen to know if he took a shower that morning before the show," said Daniel sarcastically.

Mara stopped, put her hands on her hips and glared at him. She was getting pissed. She tried cracking her neck like she had seen in Bruce Lee movies lots of times (without actually managing to crack anything), closed her eyes slightly and frowned. Noa had never seen her that angry before, so she was getting ready to grab her by the arm if she had to.

"Listen up, Daniel. As a person who only whines, complains and destroys things, what do you want to be when you grow up? I'm curious. *Really* curious."

"I was jo—"

"You're always joking!" said Mara, cutting him off. "It's your way of not dealing with things. I don't care if you don't like Michael Jackson. Just like you don't like learning things, playing sports, reading, walking... What *do* you like? Apart from eating ice-cream and playing videogames."

"I like..."

"Nothing!" yelled Mara, cutting him off once again. "You only like stuff that lets you slack off, or show off something pointless. Basically, living life with absolutely no goals."

Noa wanted the ground to swallow her up. She awkwardly smiled at people who were walking by staring at the scene the two of them were making. Maybe Mara was going a bit overboard. Noa also agreed that Daniel should be a bit more proactive and less whiney, but they were on vacation and this wasn't something new. They both knew what Daniel was like and they had learned to love him just the way he was.

"Fine, smarty-pants. Screw you! I'm out," cried Daniel.

He turned around, hands in pockets, and began walking towards the southern part of Manhattan, not really knowing where he was headed.

"Sure, just walk away! That's very mature of you..." said Mara, who began to lower her voice. She began to feel a bit guilty about yelling at her friend in public.

Mara and Noa briefly exchanged looks. Mara knew she had overreacted.

She was going through a tough time. She didn't want to admit it, but maybe she needed help. It wasn't all about learning and setting milestones on a map with a marker. Vacations were also a great opportunity to relax, meditate and, of course, play. Even if her brain was more advanced and it was able to absorb new knowledge easier, at the end of the day she was still a preteen dealing with a difficult situation.

She suddenly realized she was neck-deep in a dynamic where she kept her head busy with any sort of daily activity, regardless of how simple it was. In order to avoid thinking of things that scared her, she created her own problems that would lead her brain to a place of false security.

Her brain didn't have a moment's rest. With all the places they had to visit, all the breakfast and lunch breaks with her mother and friends, and professor Marley's classes, there was barely any time left for what was really bugging her: uncle Arnold's whereabouts.

And if she didn't want to look for her uncle alone, she needed to control her temper. She wasn't used to fighting with Noa or Daniel, especially not in an aggressive manner. She was worried that Daniel might not want to be part of their group anymore, and worried that she might eventually lose Noa too.

After walking for a while longer they reached *Bethel Gospel Assembly*, a must-see at 1832 Madison Avenue for those who wanted to experience an incredible gospel mass. Both girls went inside, walked to the top area and sat down in the back, where it looked like tourists would sit.

There was a large piece of wood above the stage with letters that read "Holiness Unto the Lord." They spent the next three hours enjoying the incredible performance. Lots of people went on and off the stage. Some yelled at the sky, others at the crowd, and many others at the microphone. They asked for amazing things for the living, the dead, and those who were yet to come into this world.

"I think they've covered just about everything in their prayers, huh?" whispered Noa into Mara's ear.

The mass was just about to end. Some parts of what they had just experienced felt more like a concert than going to church. On their way out, they both thought of Ms. Wright. They hadn't talked about her in weeks, but seeing this gospel reminded them of her. She would have really enjoyed herself.

"Don't you think she might be taken aback with all the singing and dancing?" asked Noa.

"Maybe. She's more into quiet masses and spiritual retreats."

"What's a spiritual retreat?"

"It's when people go to an isolated place without computers or mobile phones, and don't speak for days. She said she sometimes does that because it renews her body and soul, or something like that," explained Mara.

"Daniel would die in a place like that. No talking, no videogames... Do they have food?"

"Yeah, I think they have food. But pretty basic stuff. Just enough to stay alive. Remember their priority is getting close to God, that's why it's called spiritual retreat..."

They both started walking back and reached the other side of Manhattan. They had agreed to meet Sandra at Battery Park, close to where the Twin Towers had been before the attack on September 11th, 2001. Now there was a nice park and two beautiful fountains with the names of all those who died carved into the black marble, and a museum. There was also another new building now: One World Trade Center. It was huge and beautiful, with a giant antenna at the top.

"Maybe that antenna's high enough to detect where my uncle's radio signal came from," thought Mara while looking up at the building, trying to block the sun from her eyes with her hand. Daniel wasn't there. He probably decided to go back to the Museum of Natural History to try and touch a T-rex bone, then take a picture to show his friends back in Liverpool.

"Maybe this time he won't get yelled at by a security guard for trying to touch a dinosaur bone," Noa told Sandra Hopper, who was laughing at Daniel's museum adventures.

"But he wanted more than to just touch bones. He also wanted a selfie so he could show off back in school," added Mara. "Doubt he'll brag about wandering off alone this morning, though."

Noa didn't like how Mara justified their friend's absence, but she also knew that Mara didn't want to worry her mother. The three of them ate while Sandra was looking through all the things she got that day around Wall Street.

"Did you know that the One World Trade Center cost about 4 billion dollars to build?" she said, surprised, while looking at the bold printed text on a pamphlet.

"Wow, that's an insane amount of money," claimed Mara, trying to hide the fact that she really didn't care about what her mother was saying.

Her brain was currently split into two: she felt guilty about her fight with Daniel and she was eager to go back to Alex Marley's garage. Not only was it the place where they went to learn about programming, but also it was the last place where she'd heard *his* voice.

When they arrived at Alex's house, Daniel was already there. He had gotten there a few minutes before. He had a Yankees cap on and was holding a bag full of things he bought. He was also wearing a new pair of shoes.

"Looks like you really made the most of your day, huh?" Noa said to Daniel, trying to keep herself from laughing.

"Yeah, and I also got you guys a gift. Although you don't deserve it," he said reaching into his bag, smiling.

He pulled out two shoeboxes. Mara and Noa looked at the boxes before opening them.

"So, they're... D'Originals? Is that some sort of New York brand?" asked Noa out of curiosity.

"No clue, but I saw some kids wearing them and asked where they got them. So, I decided to get you guys a pair. Although you *really* don't deserve them..."

"Thanks, Daniel! They're the prettiest undeserved shoes I've ever had!" said Mara while holding up her colorful patterned shoes. "You've also probably run out of cash too, right? By the way, did you get to touch the T-rex yet?"

Noa burst out laughing and Daniel, who was expecting Mara to bring that up again, answered with his squeaky voice.

"*By the way, did you get to touch the T-rex yet?* And yeah, I'm basically poor now. I guess I'll have to ask Mrs. Hopper for a loan."

They walked into their classroom.

"What do you guys want to discuss today before learning about the world of cryptograph…?" Alex Marley began to ask.

"Hacking!" claimed Daniel with great enthusiasm, not letting him finish his question.

"Uh, sure. Mara, you'll position yourself against it because I know that, in reality, you're in favor. And, Daniel, you'll have to defend it. Noa, you'll be watching your friends this round."

Since day two, Mr. Marley had taught them the importance of debating, communicating and speaking correctly. Why was this so important? Because in order to speak properly, it was essential to know how to conceptualize, be able to take a larger idea and break it down into smaller ones, and expressing them in an orderly manner while keeping the listener interested.

Those who didn't know how to express their curiosities or had none at all, who just listened to what they were being told without reacting in any way to the information they received were bound to be programmed (or hacked). And that didn't sound too good.

"Hacking is a discipline inside the context of computer science that isn't regulated, so it's basically open to unwanted individuals…" said Mara in order to begin the debate.

"Hang on, Mara. You're using a pejorative adjective to describe a group of people without any prior arguments to back it up. Remember, starting a debate by denigrating someone or something isn't the best choice," Professor Marley explained while Noa and Daniel took notes on what he was saying.

"You're right, I'll start over."

"We're all ears," he replied.

"Hacking isn't something you study in school and it's not monitored by anyone. Anyone who knows how to hack and has a mental dis… has an internal disorder could be a potential danger for everyone. We live in a world with hundreds of millions of 'hackable' devices, so the chances of computers getting cyberattacked are pretty high. Therefore, all the different governments should work together to make sure all crackers are being watched properly."

Mara's explanation was short and simple, and everyone was quite curious as to what Daniel had to say about it. He was still taking notes on what Mara had said.

"I'm surprised you said that, Mara!" replied Daniel, lifting one eyebrow and pointing his index finger up to the ceiling as he had seen politicians do on television. "Hackers are actually people who help our society grow, since they see our reality from a different perspective."

Daniel's reply to Mara's initial statement was surprisingly good. Everyone kept on listening carefully.

"Where you may see a microwave, a hacker sees a device with a small processor they can use to control the time they need to make popcorn… or to make a robot for something else! Everyone else, the 'programmed', only see a metal box they use to warm up their milk in the morning. They stare at it sleepily waiting for the timer to go *DING*. Do you see why hackers are so important in society?"

"To turn a microwave into a robot?" Mara replied, although she was impressed at what Daniel had just explained.

"To see beyond what they want us to see!" he said excitedly. "The government and large companies are the ones that program us. They're the ones that hack us. If we're aware that there's more than meets the eye and are critical about it, we could counterprogram and help build a better world with points of view that may vary from those imposed upon us."

Mara was at a loss for words. She got up from her chair, walked up to Daniel and gave him a big hug. She was so proud of him.

"Hey, you're squishing me!"

Despite his whining, Daniel was smiling and blushing. His smart friend was proud of him.

Noa and Alex were watching them with a smile. All that was left was for Daniel to fully understand the importance of everything they were learning that summer in Alex's garage. After everyone finished congratulating Daniel, Alex Marley began explaining what cryptography was and its relevance in a world where machines could communicate with each other.

"The Internet was designed so computers could be connected with each other on a network. When a computer is connected, it's assigned a unique address through which it can be located: the IP address. An IP address is a number that's assigned to any electronic device with a CPU and is used to access it," explained Alex right before turning on the big monitor behind him.

"So, anyone can access my computer if they know my IP?" asked Noa, worried about having a device that could be used by other people.

"In theory, yes. Where do you think all the information about your daily activity is saved?"

"I don't know, Professor Marley. In my phone's memory in the form of ones and zeroes?"

"Yes... and no. If that information was only saved on your phone memory, you wouldn't get daily recommendations on where to go, how many calories you should eat or which of your friends are walking more miles than you."

The three kids stayed quiet for a minute, thinking about the trail of information they were leaving behind them. Data, data and more data that was collected through different components of the phone and shared with computers that were thousands of miles away. And they already knew where this data went and how it was processed in order to later offer them products, services or just manipulate their wishes.

"Now imagine that information was just out there, simple ones and zeroes," Alex explained. "Anyone who managed to intercept your device and the computer where all the information was being sent..."

"...Could access my entire life without me realizing it!" Mara said, both surprised and worried.

The three kids now changed their perspective on how they shared their personal information.

"Exactly. Your entire life would be easily accessible if it weren't for cryptography."

He carried on explaining what that was. First, he gave them a short history lesson. He explained the first hieroglyphs done by the Egyptians and the origin of the word: *kryptos*, which also meant 'hide' in Greek, and *gráphein*, 'writing'. So, cryptography meant hidden writing. He carried on explaining how message encryption evolved throughout the years up until the 20th century.

"The objective was always the same, which is creating a system through which someone could communicate without fear of a third party intercepting the message and reading it. For example, Noa, what does this say?"

Professor Marley pressed a button and the following appeared on the screen.

RETPOCILEH

"No idea, professor," she replied.

"It's 'helicopter' backwards!" said Mara, excited because she managed to figure it out.

"Well done. In this case, the encryption is pretty simple. You write the word or the message backwards," professor Marley explained.

"That's a dumb system, anyone can figure out what it says," Daniel said out loud.

Alex Marley grinned and pressed the button once again. The screen changed and showed the following.

KHOLFRSWHU

"That looks like a German word, right?" asked Daniel, looking at Mara and Noa, seeking their approval.

"Nope, it still says 'helicopter'. But it's encoded differently. This one's called *Caesar cipher*. Each letter is replaced by the one that's three positions ahead in the alphabet."

The three kids stared at the screen in amazement. They thought they had found a foolproof option, but Professor Marley burst their bubble.

"This sort of encryption was used by Julius Caesar to communicate important military messages. And it was still used up until the last century! In fact, it was still used in 1915 by the Russian navy, who thought it was more appropriate for their troops compared to other systems that were much more complicated. But, because it was simpler, it was beneficial for German and Austrian cryptanalysts. They easily figured out what they were up to."

"Man, that sucks..." said Daniel.

"Caesar cipher is too easy to figure out. If someone realized that they're using this type of encryption method, they just need to try out 26 different replacements. Just as many letters as there are in the alphabet. So, figuring out what the message says is pretty trivial, you see?"

The three of them nodded, eyes wide open. They wanted to know more, although they weren't too sure how cryptography could be useful for them. There wasn't a lot of information they needed to hide from the rest of the world, they were only kids after all. Or, at least that's what they thought...

"More interesting facts! During World War II, something extremely important happened. A mathematician from London managed to decipher the encrypted communication among the Nazis thanks to his creation called the *Bombe*. It was like a computer that worked like the *Enigma machine*," explained the professor.

"Enigma machine?" asked Noa.

"Yes. It's the machine the Germans used to hide their war plans from the Allies of World War II. Hitler's forces had gotten used to exchanging information on a daily basis which they processed through this machine. That way, it was invisible for anyone else. Although sometimes their messages were intercepted, nobody knew what they said. This was until Alan Turing designed a machine that managed to recreate the Enigma's behavior."

"Hey! His last name's Turing, just like me! Do you think we're related? Maybe he's my great grandpa or something…" said Mara.

"Maybe you can try researching your family tree, Mara. You might be in for a surprise!" replied Alex Marley. "Thanks to that man, the Second World War lasted two to four years less than what they had predicted, and avoided over three million casualties. The Allies anticipated the bombings from the Axis, or enemies, who didn't even know the Bombe existed until several decades later."

Another afternoon went by where the three kids listened carefully to everything their professor was teaching them. They'd only known each other for a few weeks, but something about him made them feel as if they'd always known him.

"Symmetric and asymmetric cryptography was born by the end of the past century, and they're one of the most used systems today. Cryptography investigation has always evolved thanks to the interest it attracts from the military. But that's a different story you might not be ready for yet. It's a bit confusing. You'd still need to learn a bunch more about math to understand what I'm talking about. And that's why going to class is important if you want to be a programmer!"

"Man, what a bummer. I thought I'd have to drop out of school to be a hacker and spend the day locked up in my basement looking at a giant screen with lots of words while eating pizza, getting fat, collecting geeky things…" said Daniel, making them all laugh out loud.

Their moment of fun was interrupted by a metallic sound inside the garage. Something could be heard from the loudspeaker hanging on the wall.

"Mara, I need you to get a transmitter so we can communicate. I'm sure you can remember three numbers and letters (400nkc). I'll use simple encryption that you'll manage to understand. You'll be able to figure out when and where we'll meet up. You might be in danger. Over and out."

Everyone just stared in shock. The voice coming out of that loudspeaker was very intense. Maybe it sounded metallic and rough because the signal was low-quality. But what was clear is that someone wanted more solid contact with Mara Turing. Plus, they were talking about encryption in the middle of their lesson on that same subject. Almost as if someone were eavesdropping. That seemed highly unlikely, though, since there were no microphones in the garage and they all assumed Alex Marley was using something to cut off whatever happened in that garage from the rest of the world.

Mara got very nervous. Not only because that voice had reminded her why they were in New York and, more specifically, in that garage, but because she was going to get bombarded with lots of questions.

"Damn, your uncle…"

"Daniel, watch your language! But… damn! Can't he use something more normal? Like, a phone. This is creeping me out…" Noa said shakily.

"Quit saying the D word. Let's calm down, being nervous won't help us," said Professor Marley while pacing around, one hand at his hip and the other one scratching his head.

"We need that transmitter," blurted Mara. "And to figure out the meaning of that code he had… he just told me."

Alex Marley stopped pacing. He looked as if he had just figured something out. He widened his eyes and got closer to Mara.

"Mara, tell us everything you know. And when I say *everything*, I mean that part about 'I'm sure you remember'. Re-member? You can only remember something you knew previously. What are you hiding?"

Mara looked around, but her friends only shrugged, looking pretty confused. She had also lied to them.

"Alright, fine. I lied to you guys… I lied to get you here."

Noa and Daniel looked at each other. Then they both turned to Alex Marley. They had no idea what was going on for the past five minutes. How long had their friend been lying to them? They knew she'd do anything to see her uncle again, but they had never lied to each other when it came to serious matters.

"I appreciate you admitting it, Mara," said the professor. "Now, care to explain why?"

Arnold Turing's niece went all the way back to her childhood. She told them everything about her first years, how close she was with her uncle and how one day he just disappeared, and how that event had scarred her for life. She went on talking about all her restless nights up until that day when she heard a voice in her headphones in music class at Saint Michael.

She also explained how it was her uncle who specifically told her not to tell anyone about their plans when he contacted her through the tablet. When she saw both of her best friends at the airport, the excitement she felt about having them go to New York with her overcame the uncertainty of how to include them in her secret plans.

"I was gonna do this alone. I just needed to learn how to program, hack and so on with Professor Marley's help. My uncle would eventually contact me and tell me what to do… But I promise I wasn't expecting any of this. I don't know…"

Mara was stumbling over her words. She tried to seem convincing, but it sounded more like she was trying to say sorry to her friends.

"So, all this time I've been teaching you the basics of being a hacker, yet you've already mastered the part about manipulating," said Alex Marley jokingly. "We could have skipped the first few classes!"

"We were lied to as well, this was pretty unexpected," added Noa. "But we know how bad you want to find your uncle."

"We could be slackin' off all day, going for walks, shopping, going to the movies… anything! But no, we code, learn some history, debate, code some more… No offense, Professor. I mean, I've gotta admit I do like some of these classes."

After Daniel's complaint, the garage went silent. The sounds of the computer fans and the cars outside were the only background noise.

"I'm truly sorry. I had no other option. I've been lying to you guys for weeks and I know that's wrong. I wouldn't have been able to do this without you, I'm sure of that. And look at how much we've learned!" exclaimed Mara.

"And all that's still left to learn…" said Daniel in a distressed tone.

"Exactly, Daniel. But we're on the right track, whether it's a coincidence, destiny or because my uncle wanted it this way. Nobody will program us and *we* will determine our own future. Help me find my uncle! Not only would that make me extremely happy, but we're going to experience an unforgettable adventure together. And that includes you, Professor."

Professor Marley went quiet for a few seconds, creating both a feeling of fear and anticipation, until he broke the silence once again.

"I can get you that transmitter, Mara. But you'll need to set up an antenna in a high spot. New York is full of saturated signals."

Mara sighed in relief and felt all her muscles relax. Noa hugged her and Daniel put his index finger next to his temple, as if telling Mara that she was nuts.

Their professor walked to a shelf and grabbed a small suitcase that had a radio transmitter inside. He had restored it himself after buying it in a garage sale. He set it next to Mara while thinking about how to explain to her how careful she had to be.

"Mara, listen closely. I know you're excited about contacting your uncle right now, but I need you to be cautious. You've never stopped to even consider the chance of..." Alex was trying to find a way to put it lightly. "I mean, maybe it's not really him, or maybe he's become a totally different person. Or maybe he's being manipulated by some sort of criminal!"

Daniel started feeling extremely nervous, so he tried to go back to talking about the antenna and make a joke of it to cope with the situation.

"Maybe you can climb up the Empire State building, just like King Kong, and set the antenna up there. I think that's high enough."

"I'm not going to worry about setting it in a super high place, Daniel. My uncle wants to talk to me, so he'll figure out a way to have the signal reach me," she said.

Professor Marley watched them talk for a bit before insisting, once again, that they should consider every option as far as Arnold Turing's intentions are concerned.

"Don't rush things, Mara. What if he's not acting freely? What if he tries to hurt you?"

"Are you saying my uncle wants to *hurt me*?"

"No, I'm saying you should think about it for a few days before making a decision. We can all brainstorm together and analyze all the information we've got, and find a way to avoid getting tricked," said Professor Marley, trying not to hurt Mara's feelings.

"We don't have a few days! I mean, no offense, but I don't think you know who my uncle is. He's a really, really good man, and he needs help. And nobody's gonna keep me from finding him, alright?"

Alex was about to continue with the conversation but Noa dissuaded him with a quick gesture. Mara closed her notebook, shoved it into her backpack and hastily walked out of the garage, not wanting to hear any more of what any of them might have to say. She took the suitcase with the transmitter as well. It was quite heavy, but she grabbed it with such energy it almost seemed as if it were empty.

Mara walked to the nearest subway station and got on the next train to Manhattan. After giving it all some thought, she began to regret storming out of that garage. But she couldn't get why Alex Marley and her friends didn't understand that her uncle was a nice man who was isolated and needed their help. Why did they want to keep her away?

After spending the entire afternoon walking around Manhattan, she decided to go back home. That day she hadn't marked anything on a guide or notebook. She wandered on her own, enjoying the beauty of the city lights, the different smells, the different sounds. Mara told herself, walking around without a specific destination isn't really wasting time. She learned that it was great for letting your mind roam and notice smaller details which would usually go unnoticed. She stopped to have a milkshake from a stand on 42nd Street and enjoyed the well-known *Manhattanhenge*, which is the famous sunset between skyscrapers.

She got onto the "E" train and made her way back to Long Island City. She walked down the station stairs and continued until she reached the apartment. Her head wouldn't stop spinning. What would she tell her mom about ditching her friends? Should she tell her about her uncle trying to communicate with her? No, she couldn't possibly do that. She'd already told enough people, despite her uncle telling her not to.

All these questions kept popping up in her head until she was almost out of breath. Anxiety, again. The school's psychologist had told her several times that she needed to stop anticipating all of her problems. But that was easier said than done.

She leaned onto a street light to catch her breath. From there she could see the entrance to the building, so she began to count floors until she reached the one they were on. Every window had a light on. "I'm dead meat," she thought to herself. Her heart felt like it was about to break out of her chest.

Suddenly, Mara remembered something Daniel had said before about climbing the Empire State building like King Kong and setting up the antenna all the way on top.

"That's it!" said Mara out loud, smiling broadly allowing her nervousness to change to excitement.

She went in through the building's main door. As soon as she walked in, she saw her friends sitting on the stairs. They hadn't gone back up to the apartment so Sandra wouldn't ask questions they wouldn't know how to answer. Mara felt the guilt weigh on her shoulders, which were already tired enough as they were from carrying the suitcase around all day.

"Hey, Mara. Where've you been?" Noa asked with a worried look.

"I can't really explain right now, but I need you to come with me to the rooftop. I found a way to install the transmitter and talk to my uncle."

Noa turned to look at Daniel, who raised his eyebrows and shrugged, as if saying that they really didn't have much of a choice.

They walked up the stairs until they reached the door that, thankfully, wasn't locked. The rooftop floor was black and covered by some sort of insulation, and there were several abandoned items. A bike with flat tires, a picnic table and chairs, and an old barbeque that looked like it had been used recently.

The air vents rose high above their heads, making it look like something out of "Mary Poppins." Mara was looking around to figure out where she could install the antenna. She saw there were four brick columns from which air from the lower floors came out of. She grabbed one of the old stools next to the barbeque and moved it next to the column that was behind the rooftop entrance. It was the perfect spot to hide the metal rod that would give the device the strong signal it needed. She attached it using a rusty piece of wire that surrounded the vent.

She unrolled the antenna cable all the way onto the ground where the suitcase with the transmitter was. They needed a source of energy for it to work, so Noa and Daniel began to look for an outlet. They found one right behind the air vent. A green light turned on in the top right corner of the device. Ready! Now they just needed to wait for Mara's uncle to contact her.

"I miss you, uncle Arnold. Give me a sign, say anything! I want to see you," she thought. The only sound coming from the radio was the expected static. They were pretty confused about all the buttons on that machine. It was much more complicated than the simple interfaces they were used to.

"I don't get how they could use these things before," said Daniel out loud while looking up the instructions for that specific transmitter online: EQTAC-1958. "I'm sure the Roman Empire used it! It says 1958 because it's the year it was made in."

"It surely was faster than sending a homing pigeon or another person to the neighboring town…" said Noa. She was looking at the transmitter very closely, as if it were about to reveal more information about itself just by staring at it.

"Volume is set to half. I'm gonna press this button that says 'Band' and I'll move this wheel left and right. What do I press first, Daniel? Come on, you choose something for once. Something that's not an ice-cream flavor," said Mara, looking back and up at her friend, who was still looking for instructions on his phone.

"Wow, nice try at recovering our broken relationship. Move it all the way to the right," he replied.

"Mara, just so you know… we're with you 'till the end, OK? If life has pushed you to live this difficult adventure and we're part of your life… it doesn't take a genius to know that we'll stick together no matter what."

"Thanks, Noa" said Mara excitedly. "I'm counting on you guys. I know you've got my back. Now I need to figure out what those three letters and numbers that my uncle said have to do with this machine. It was… 400nkc."

Their conversation, however, was not as private as they thought.

"Do not fret, Mara! If you cannot find the formula, I will assist you [affirmation]," Hermes added to its log file, which it used as a diary.

Chapter 12

IT'S TIME

A S the sun began to set, the first rays of light shone through Falko McKinnon's cell windows in Hidden Peak. Hermes always waited until the sun began to set. It was the most optimal time for communicating with Falko using their special system.

The prisoner grabbed his paper and pencil and got ready to take notes. A fine yet powerful laser was responsible for the presence or absence of a spot of light on both glasses. One and zero, respectively.

McKinnon's replies were also quite complex. He would cover and uncover the small windows to communicate with Hermes in a similar way. However, it was much more complicated when having to use the light from the torches inside the prison.

It was a very slow system, and it was very important that the windows were clean. It was also important that the focus was correct, which was also difficult since the one in charge of managing the communication system was an artificial intelligence with no limbs. "Once I get out of here, I'll implement another system that's quicker than this one. Compressing the signal would be nice. Why didn't I think of that before?" he thought to himself while taking notes of what Hermes was saying.

"Good job, Hermes. I knew your code was superior, but sometimes you truly amaze me. You're insane. You even scare me."

Hermes had sent the following message using 8-bit blocks in binary:

01000011 01101111 01101101 01110000 01110101
01110100 01101001 01101110 01100111 00100000
01110000 01101111 01110011 01110011 01101001
01100010 01101100 01100101 00100000 01110011
01101111 01101100 01110101 01110100 01101001
01101111 01101110 01110011 00100000 01110100
01101111 00100000 01101101 01110101 01110010
01100100 01100101 01110010 00100000 01001101
01100001 01110010 01100001 00100000 01010100
01110101 01110010 01101001 01101110 01100111
00100000 01100001 01101110 01100100 00100000
01101011 01100101 01100101 01110000 01101001
01101110 01100111 00100000 01101000 01100101
01110010 00100000 01100110 01110010 …

Falko knew the equivalents by heart, so he was translating
on the go…

> *Computing possible solutions to murder Mara Turing
> and preventing her from deciphering our secret document.
> Creator, allow me to express something more 'human':
> sometimes I feel like an evil machine, programmed with
> dark and harmful objectives that affect many individuals.
> But I have learned something while checking my source
> code. 'Human', 'evil', 'dark' and 'harmful' are adjectives
> that sometimes lead someone into a spiral of thoughts that
> keep them from fulfilling their goals. However, I am not a
> human.*

Falko began to reply immediately. The prison torches would turn off at 10 p.m. each night and would be turned back on at 5 p.m. the following day. During summer, his communication window with Hermes was much shorter: there'd be no light until 7:30 p.m.

"OK, Hermes. Continue with your plan. Thanks for taking care of our mission," said Falko to his creation before going back to bed. He laid back and looked up at the ceiling, hands behind his head. He smiled, thinking about how the niece of the Dirtee Loopers' biggest traitor would soon pass on to a better life.

"I hope she doesn't suffer too much. She's only a kid, after all. And it's not her fault her uncle's a coward. She's also not responsible for her inherited intelligence. I should've mentioned it: make it quick and painless... Oh well, it'll choose whatever it thinks is best without any prejudgment or, as Hermes puts it, *adjectives*," Falko thought to himself before falling asleep.

On the other side of the world, several thousand miles from Queens, Hermes was running calculations in an abandoned data center. When you travel through cables at the speed of light, a thousand kilometers can be travelled in much less than a second. It had processed around a hundred million different solutions to the issue "Kill Mara Turing", but chances would be much higher if other humans were to help.

But how would someone cooperate with Hermes? Simple: they would help execute the calculations much faster. The data center where the AI was located was very old, so any mobile device today is more powerful than any of the computers there.

McKinnon's creation had installed itself on the most powerful computer available. It dumped its code into it and tried to obtain an optimal configuration. However, despite having changed hundreds of things around and moving its modules hundreds of times, it could never get all the resources it needed to go faster.

But the limited power wasn't the only issue. If it were to use up all the CPUs and available memory, it would risk being detected by slowing down (or maybe even crashing) all the systems that were connected to that data center.

"If I were human, this would be a time to cry. But, luckily, I am not [laugh]," wrote Hermes on its log file before setting this last issue to one side and searching for an alternative for the lack of processing power.

It had several dangerous ideas before coming up with the least offensive option for itself. Any online game with a ranking system and through which users could compete with friends would be a great candidate. And that's what happened with Diamonds Bombing Party II, a multi-platform app that could be used on any device, such as a smartwatch, a phone or even a car's entertainment system.

Hermes had calculated that there were about 1 billion machines (phones, computers, tablets, watches…) that were potentially hackable. Out of all those, 300 million were hard to attack because they belonged to Pear Factory, one of the most important hardware and software manufacturers known for having great protection against cyberattacks. Another

100 million didn't have an Internet connection, which made it impossible to inject malicious code into them since they weren't accessible.

In a matter of seconds, Hermes managed to find a copy of the Diamonds Bombing Party II files with the original code on a Russian server. They contained the exact recipe used to program the game for all those different platforms. In about 15 minutes it found three vulnerabilities to exploit. In other words, in around a quarter of an hour Falko McKinnon's AI managed to find three security breaches that would allow it to use this game to infiltrate over 600 million processors.

Hermes came up with an easy system for this. It would trick the applications center Binary into thinking there's a new update, which would then open a back door into Diamonds Bombing Party II. This way, it would get into all those devices without the users knowing it. While the app was running in the background, it would be calculating non-stop.

This wasn't something new Hermes had discovered. Thousands of people accidentally allow viruses on their computers, phones and watches by doing simple things such as opening a seemingly harmless e-mail or a picture sent by a friend. What was truly impressive was the speed at which Hermes had begun to work at.

And that's how on August 25th of 2013, half of planet Earth had their devices calculating for Hermes without even knowing it.

"Every computation cycle I go through, the less I understand how humans are not extinct. They create powerful things, yet they do not verify them correctly [reflection]," it wrote on the log file. It felt its brain expand. In a matter of hours, its processing capacity reached the never-before-seen amount of 10 *octillion* operations per second.

"Not even with this power would we be able to solve Tic-tack-toe. These silly humans like to create things that do not make sense [sarcasm]," Hermes wrote once again. For the past few days, Hermes had begun to add more information about its *sensations*, and this is something that not even Falko McKinnon knew about.

That day, nobody noticed that Diamonds Bombing Party II was running a bit slower than usual. Not only because it was hard to tell, but because people who play this game are usually too focused on matching colored diamonds on their screen non-stop.

Only fifteen hours later, Hermes had figured out the most optimal solution to its problem. The common denominator in almost all of its simulations was the same: killing Mara Turing, as well as testing how smart she really was. This last part was a decision it had made on its own.

It really wanted to find a human being that could provide a clue on what that secret document contained. Falko hadn't even managed to find a meaning to the file itself.

Hermes still had the file which Falko had accessed years ago, and still remains an absolute mystery. It tried hundreds of different encodings: common ones, unknown ones, some created *ad hoc* by trying to anticipate future technologies or interpreting ones from several centuries ago.

Nothing worked.

All hopes were set on a single string of text: 3RDI.

What did 3RDI stand for? Nobody knew. Hermes and Falko had tried everything they could come up with and everything was still exactly the same as that night in which they found an unexpected file while mounting a cyber attack on the website of the "World's safest bank". Soteria World Bank (SWB) had been a huge target for crackers all over the world. That was all thanks to some wise guy from the marketing department who decided to include this tag line in every single ad: "Bring all your money to the one place it surely won't leave… if you don't want it to […] Soteria World Bank, the safest place for your savings."

Cyberattacks multiplied by a thousand in a matter of hours. SWB had a very secure network thanks to hundreds of computers distributed throughout the world. The infrastructure had been designed by Donnie Shimomura, a white-collar hacker with an impressive background. There wasn't anything he hadn't been able to hack into in the last 25 years.

He, just like many other hackers, began with Blue boxes[7], reading fanzines and guides he got off the black market. He idolized crazy scientists and spent hundreds of hours typing away in front of a computer screen. And, just like many other hackers, he turned into a cracker when he least expected it and without knowing who he was doing the dirty work for.

They had asked him through normal mail to access a Chinese university database to edit the marks of a couple of students

---

7. *A blue box is an electronic device used to generate tones through a telephone line. It's used as a phone phreaking or hacking tool.*

who were brothers. The reward was pretty juicy if he managed to do it, and there wasn't much risk as the relationship between China and the United States wasn't really good. If authorities were to catch him red-handed, they wouldn't extradite him to a communist country. So, he accepted.

He managed to do it in record time and within 48 hours of accomplishing the task, he received a check at his home big enough to buy half a videogame store. After he completed his first job, he started getting riskier ones. Shimomura had a solid code of ethics, so he never accepted any job that could put lives at risk.

However, on a night like any other, when he thought he was an almighty yet invisible being, he came across Tony Mitnick while digging through a London hospital's database of VIP clients.

The rest of the story is public and pretty much well-known. The authorities offered him the chance to join the good guys and, in exchange, receive a reduced sentence. Shimomura accepted immediately and began to work for the Government. With time, he got bored of a job that wasn't challenging at all. And that's how he moved onto private companies, although before doing so he had to do a few more favors in order to be set completely free. After that, he ended up at SWB, which is where he came up with the best security system he had ever made.

The best until Falko and Hermes came along, that is.

Thousands of hackers and crackers had tried relentlessly to access the SWB network but never succeeded. Their peak had been 100 attacks per second. "It's like hitting a sort of endless wall. An infinite barrier. Shimomura's system seemed almost perfect, and the most common attack methods were totally useless. Brute force[8], trojans, worms[9], keyloggers[10]…" explained a modest Italian hacker to World News TV. He had agreed to do the interview, on condition of anonymity, almost immediately after someone finally managed to successfully hack into the SWB network.

Falko McKinnon had bragged about it being one of the easiest jobs he had ever done. He uploaded data from millions of clients to a server on the Deep Web with a note that read:

Shimomura is just a rusty old programmer with a bit of luck. My partner and I found a flaw in the system in no time. All you had to do was learn a little about Shimomura's life. Right, Donnie?

After all that boasting, Falko (who, by the way, didn't steal money, he only leaked data) disconnected everything to focus on something that had caught his attention that day. The Shimomura fortress inside the SWB network had several files with a never-before-seen encryption. Although these documents were split into smaller pieces, spread out among computers throughout the world, Hermes managed to piece it all back together.

---

8. *A brute-force attack is when an attacker attempts all possible password combinations until they find the correct one.*
9. *A computer worm is a computer virus that can replicate in order to spread onto other computers.*
10. *Program used for hacking through which the attacker can capture the key strokes of their victim.*

Some of those files had the same prefix in their name ("3RDI") followed by a line of alphanumeric text that didn't seem to have any meaning. Every file was exactly the same size and inside each of them were several large blank sections.

For the next few hours, Falko and Hermes made an effort to decipher the content of their discovery. It took them a couple of hours to figure out the documents that were encrypted with SUEA-1024 (*Shimomura's Unbreakable Encryption Algorithm*). However, when he attempted to see what was in those files, he realized that the ones starting with "3RDI" were still unreadable. Falko completely ignored all the other data he had just gained access to and focused completely on those mysterious files.

Hours went by and there were no breakthroughs. Falko thought maybe it was due to the fact that he was already mentally exhausted, so he had decided to go to sleep after being up for 54 hours straight, hacking non-stop. He left Hermes working on possible ways to extract information from those files. He was sure that his restless AI, which didn't even have to stop to sleep or eat (unlike him) would do the necessary work. He expected he would wake up to the 6 monitors in the middle of his apartment full of information from those files.

But that never happened.

Falko McKinnon was extremely frustrated for days. He, the best hacker, cracker and programmer to ever exist, wasn't able to find anything in that mess of data. He tried everything he could think of, and he encouraged Hermes to predict what he was yet to know about the world of encryption.

He read through all the information he could find in every computer Donnie Shimomura ever owned since he was a child. There was nothing on any encryption algorithm that would help him figure out what was in those files. Hermes even suggested he should go out and find Shimomura. "Torture him if necessary. He must know the encryption in these files [suggestion]," the AI added to its log file.

They never found the right time or way. One thing would be catching Shimomura off-guard, but another thing was thinking he was clueless. Since then, they were never able to get remotely close to him, neither physically nor electronically.

Falko had his hopes up at first, but, with time, he began to give up. Although he never really stopped thinking about those files, he began to focus on other priorities he had. He led the Dirtee Loopers during several of their attacks aimed at highlighting his more charitable, egalitarian and visionary side. And that's all they did until the famous IFV attack.

Hermes, who had played an important role in IFV by infiltrating the computer networks of the largest hardware manufacturers in the world, valued the different options Falko had presented to decrypt the files starting with 3RDI *if* he ever managed to escape from Hidden Peak.

The total number of options he had were basically none.

The AI was aware of how dangerous it would be to communicate that information to its creator, so it decided to simply write it in a log file.

Chapter 13

ENCRYPTED MESSAGE FOR MARA

NIGHTS in Queens had started to cool down despite it still being summertime. The EQTAC-1958 made weird noises and only provided the three kids with useless information. For the past half hour, Mara and her friends had heard all sorts of things from it, and lots of them weren't suitable for their age.

"So, to recap what we've heard, firefighters have rescued 10 cats around Manhattan…" said Daniel in order to break the silence.

The only thing that came out of that device was interference.

"Shhh! Quiet!" Mara hushed her friend with her index finger over her lips. "I'm sure we'll hear something. We just need to find the right frequency. And the meaning of 400nkc."

"Right…" Noa yawned and rested her head on Daniel's shoulder, who was busy looking up at a shooting star flying across the New York sky.

"Hey, get off!" jumped Daniel. "You better not have a crush on me or something. I know I'm handsome, my grandma said so. And my grandma never lies."

He was blushing.

Noa quickly got up and wiped dirt off her pants so Sandra wouldn't complain about how dirty they were.

"I'm off to bed, guys."

"Wait up, I'll go too. I think 'Cats Stuck in Trees: Part II' can wait until tomorrow," said Daniel, cleaning his pants too as he got up.

He followed Noa towards the rooftop door. Mara stayed put, smiled at her friends and barely waved at them as they headed for the staircase. She stared at her transmitter, lowered the volume a bit so she wouldn't bother the neighbors, and began to move the tuning dial left and right. She would randomly come across conversations between other people.

"KDK-1 to KDK-2, do you read me? Hahaha! You like my impression of Wendy calling the forest rangers in The Shining? Hey, you there? Emma! Please... I'll stop messing around, sorry."

Mara continued moving the dial and kept on hearing all sorts of things. Some of those things were inappropriate for her age, but she dismissed them and focused solely on finding her uncle's voice among that chaos. She realized that people communicating through these devices all used strange codenames instead of their real names. She remembered Professor Marley calling these "alphanumeric codes".

Roughly 10 minutes had passed since Mara's friends had gone to bed and all you could hear on this calm night in Queens was the predictable sounds of the subway arriving and leaving the 30th Avenue station nearby at regular 10-minute intervals. If you really paid attention, you could almost make out the conversations of people waiting for the next train. Mara felt it was getting late by the decreasing temperature and how her long-sleeve shirt was feeling thinner by the minute.

She looked up from the transmitter and realized it was not only cold but very dark on that rooftop despite the street lights below and for the first time in a long time, Mara felt scared. She started seeing shadows around her and kept turning her head left and right. She turned off the volume on the transmitter to focus on what now seemed like absolute silence in the city that seemingly never sleeps. She shivered, partly reacting to the cold and partly reacting to something she saw move at the far end of the rooftop.

"Calm down Mara, there's nobody here," she thought to herself, but not believing it either. She moved softly, trying to catch a glimpse of anything or anyone that might be on that rooftop with her.

Then a sudden *slam* made her jump. It sounded like a lid of a metal trash can crashing to the ground. Mara started shaking, and not because of the cold. She got behind the air vent where the transmitter had been placed and began to try and control her breath.

"Breathe in, two, three… breathe out, two, three, four, five…"

Before she was done counting, she saw what looked like a head ducking near the edge of the rooftop. Maybe it wasn't the best time to relax. She felt a lump in her throat and pressure on her chest.

"There's no time to get scared, Mara. Focus. 400nkc. Four hundred, N, K, C. Four, zero, zero…" she began to think out loud.

She tried to keep her voice down. Though she was sure nobody could hear her, she didn't want to seem like a psycho talking to herself.

She visualized each number in her head and created a mental map. She tried to think what her uncle would assume she had learned up until that point. Going to the garage, attending Professor Marley's classes. Knowledge, garage, code…

"What did I learn in that garage that could help me decipher this? I'm sure it's somewhere along that logic," she whispered, looking at the dial once again.

Knowledge, garage, code, transmitter… dial? She felt her reasoning was leading her down the right path. Her eyes were wandering around the transmitter when they suddenly landed on the dial scale: "Khz". Three letters.

"That's it! Three letters. N, K, C. K, H, Z."

She mentally pictured the alphabet in her head while repeating the letters over and over.

A B **C** D E F G **H** I J **K** L M **N** O P Q R S T U V W X Y **Z**

What was the distance between letters that made up "khz" and "nkc"? She counted the number of characters and came up with a hypothesis: her uncle had used something similar to Caesar Cipher. It made sense. He assumed they'd learn that in one of their first classes on cryptography and wanted to keep the puzzle simple for his niece. Three letters backwards! So, "nkc" became "khz". The last letter threw her off at first, but she immediately knew that if she got to the beginning of the alphabet, she had to start again from the end.

"A frequency! It's a frequency! That was pretty easy, Arnold Turing," said Mara, thinking of Mikey when he spoke out loud to One-Eyed Willy in *The Goonies*.

Once she figured out the codification, she did the same with the numbers. So, 400 became 177. That was the frequency: 177Khz. She turned the dial to that exact position, then waited for the magic to happen. After a few seconds, she heard a voice.

"Mara. It's me, your uncle Arnold. Can you hear me?"

She rushed to plug in the headphones she had brought with her in case that moment ever came. Mara didn't want to miss a single word her uncle had to tell her, even if that meant not being able to hear if there was anything or anyone around her. "Nothing's ever perfect," she thought while lowering the mic to her mouth. She looked back at that dark rooftop corner where something seemed to have been moving moments before. She was so tense it took her a moment to realize that her fists were clenched so hard she was digging her nails into her own palms. Her teeth were chattering, not sure if it was the cold or because she was scared.

"Yes, uncle Arnold! I-I can hear you, l-loud and clear," she replied shakily. "W-Where are you?"

"I'm so glad to hear your voice, my dear. I have so much to tell you. I know you've probably heard hundreds of stories about me. And I don't think most of them are good ones. Maybe even my sister-in-law, Sandra, tries to protect you from me. But you know I'd never hurt you. Right, Mara?"

A tear ran down her cheek. She was positive that her mother had kept everything about Arnold from her. It was the taboo subject that nobody talked about in front of little Mara. What her uncle just told her confirmed her suspicions. But now that was all in the past. She finally felt him near, and she wasn't going to let him get away this time.

"I know. You're kind… and smart! And you've got to teach me tons of things. I really admire and love you… I want to know everything about you and why my mom won't tell me about your past. When can we see each other? Tomorrow?"

"Don't get ahead of yourself. We need to meet somewhere that's not suspicious. I'll come up with a plan and I'll let you know once I have it. Do you have an e-mail address?"

She gave him the one she created in one of their classes.

"Great, Mara. I'll send over the information in the next few days. It will be encrypted, though. That way, nobody can read it. Do you think you'll be able to decipher it?"

"Of course, uncle Arnold! And, if not, I can always get professor Marley to…"

"NO!"

He raised his voice to a point where it hurt Mara's eardrums. She quickly put her hands up over the headphones and shut her eyes.

"Nobody can know about this, remember? We don't know who we can trust yet, so be quiet about it and wait."

"Alright. I'm sorry, uncle Arnold," she replied, rubbing her ear under one side of her headset. "It's just that I really want to see you. I want to hear all your stories."

"I need to disconnect now; someone could intercept our conversation and locate me. Check your e-mail tomorrow. Good night, little one."

Mara sighed deeply. A shooting star crossed over the night sky and Mara quickly made a wish for her uncle's safety while trying to hold back the tears that were welling up inside. She knew this moment would be imprinted in her memory for the rest of her life. And while she felt closer than ever to her uncle now, after deciphering the alphanumeric code, she simply couldn't wait for that next message that would get her even closer to him.

"Why are you still up here? It's cold and lonely," said Sandra Hopper after opening the rooftop door.

"Nothing, mom!" Mara replied nervously.

She wiped her eyes with her hoodie sleeve, got up and shook the dirt off her pants.

They started walking down the stairs. Mara was thinking of an excuse as to why she was still up there all by herself after midnight. The best that she could come up with was stargazing. It didn't fully convince Sandra, but she also didn't have any other reason to not trust her daughter.

Sandra had always felt slightly guilty about the technological isolation she put her daughter through. Although it was for her own good (so she wouldn't get hurt or, even worse, disappear like her uncle), she knew how hard it was for her, especially when most kids now carried phones and gadgets all day.

Mara went to grab her pajamas from the room where Noa and Daniel were sleeping soundly. There was a poster on one of the walls with several guys that looked like 80s rockers. She headed for the bathroom to change, hoping that the next several hours would just pass quickly.

Despite her anxiousness, Mara slept peacefully that night, with a smile drawn across her face. At around 8 a.m. they got up to go for another walk around the city. Sandra, Mara, Daniel and Noa were spending another morning in Manhattan. They had saved those days to explore the Upper East Side. They had breakfast at Oslo Coffee Roasters, one of the most famous coffee shops in that area.

Daniel almost cried tears of joy after trying the almond croissant. He sure wasn't going to lose weight during that trip, but he wasn't gaining it either thanks to all the walking they were doing.

Mara used those quick moments where Sandra got up to order or pay at the bar to update her friends on what had happened the night before on the rooftop. They were excited as well, but also warned her to be careful, just in case.

They continued with their walk until they reached the Roosevelt Island tramway on 59th Street and Second Avenue. Once they got on it and began to move, they had the entire East River under their feet. Time to visit Roosevelt Island! They'd seen it several times from Queens and they were really eager to finally step foot on it.

As soon as they got off, Mara started taking pictures of the Manhattan view. She pulled her map out.

"We've got over ten different places to see here!"

She walked up to her friends and they began planning their route for that day. She couldn't wait to check her e-mail that afternoon, but had to control her obvious nervousness. She tried her best to calm down and not create suspicion, and so she decided to enjoy that afternoon in a not-so-famous part of the city and focus on the email when she could finally read it.

"Let's go north first and check out the Blackwell Island Lighthouse," suggested Mara. "From there we'll walk to all the other places, like the Chapel of the Good Shepherd, Blackwell House, Four Freedoms Park, Octagon and…. drumroll, please… the Smallpox Hospital ruins!"

"Aha! What do you know about that hospital?" asked Sandra looking straight at Daniel.

"Approximately zero things, Mrs. Hopper. You think I've got time to study when I haven't even had time to try all the ice-cream flavors they have here? And I discarded all the common flavors, because that would just be a waste of time…"

Sandra began laughing uncontrollably, which reminded Mara and Noa of how funny Daniel's jokes could be when you haven't heard them a thousand times.

The scenery here was quite different from what they were used to until then. Buildings weren't very tall and there were some zones of the hospital area where it seemed long-term patients stayed. An elderly man wearing light blue pajamas was staring out at Manhattan. He was in a wheelchair. A few feet from him was someone who was probably his caretaker, but who was paying more attention to his cigarette than the patient. As they kept walking, they saw similar patients who seemed lonely and longing for something more out of life.

All that apparent solitude really made the three kids stop and think. They had heard stories about people who abandon their sick or elderly family members, but they were now witnessing that painful truth in person. It was a humid August morning and thermometers barely reached 68 °F. It wasn't exactly comfortable in the shade.

Patients were hoping for the sun to bring some typical August warmth, as if they were trying to store it ahead of the cold winter months to come. Daniel, feeling uneasy by the eternal silence that fell upon his group of friends after seeing that first lonely old man, decided to break the ice. He grabbed his phone and looked up information on the hospital Sandra had asked him about before. He tried to memorize it all as fast as he could.

"So, Mrs. Hopper, what do you know about the 'haunted Roosevelt Island hospital'?" he asked with a know-it-all look across his face. He quickly tried hiding his phone in his pocket, although everyone had just seen him use it to look up information.

"What do you mean? There's no such thing as a 'haunted hospital'. Not here, not anywhere," Mara's mother answered with a confused look.

"Bzzzzz! Wrong answer, Mrs. Hopper! I see you don't know much about the hospital," Daniel replied arrogantly. "The ruins you asked me about before are actually of a ghooooost hospitaaaal."

He stretched his arms out in front of him like a mummy and opened his eyes wide.

"You're braindead, you know that? There's literally nothing in your skull. It's empty, hollow. There's probably a couple of peanuts, but that's it," blurted Noa, trying to hide the fact that she was actually scared.

"I see you're scared, but don't be ashamed…" Daniel carried on with his story, lowering his voice until it was almost a whisper. "Over fifteen hundred people died of smallpox in that hospital. All alone, abandoned. Can't you hear their screams? Also, do you think some ghosts would go around touring Manhattan eating ice-cream? Of course not! They stayed here, roaming the island…"

Sandra was trying to keep herself from laughing. Clearly, he was great at improvising an entire story based on three random facts he read a minute ago.

"…and the girls who went there in the years following when it was a training center for nurses have told terrible tales."

"Girls? And why not boys?" Mara asked, focusing on that specific detail and forcing herself not to think about ghosts.

"Up until some years ago, it was common for nurses were only female. They would only hire men as orderlies or any job that required a considerable amount of physical strength. On the other hand, doctors were exclusively men. Women weren't considered capable of handling things such as surgeries, for example…" added Sandra, knowing that her daughter would snap at this information.

And that's exactly what happened.

"That's bullcrap! Women can be whatever they want to be! Professor Marley was right, we live in an unfair world. And we should work hard to make it better, change all those unfair situations, by thinking outside the box, looking at things from a different perspective…"

"Mara, who's Professor Marley?" asked Mrs. Hopper, taken by surprise at the sound of a name she had never heard before.

Daniel quickly tried to distract Sandra from what her daughter had just said. "So, anyway, the ghosts that haunt—"

"Quiet, Daniel!" she interrupted, with her palm up facing him while she looked her daughter straight in the eyes. "I'll ask again, in case you didn't hear me: who's Professor Marley?"

She was at a dead end. Sometimes being too impulsive backfired. This was one of those times.

"Well, you see, the day we got to Queens we decided to go for a walk. Remember?"

"Get to the point!" yelled Sandra, who was nervously shaking.

She began to think that maybe that Professor Marley had something to do with the messages her daughter had received back at school.

"OK, OK! Calm down, he's not dangerous…" Mara tried calming her down.

"He's not dangerous? And how do you know that, Mara? What does he want? How long have you been seeing him? How much time have you spent with him?" Sandra started spitting out questions like a machine gun.

"He's a philosopher, studied at Stanford. He knows how to program and has a garage, which is where we've been going every afternoon since we got here. He taught us lots of things, like how to debate, being for or against a proposal, some programming, encryption…" Noa said, throwing information at Mara's mother to calm her down.

"Some programming? Encryption? I made it clear *years* ago that I wanted you to stay away from those machines. Yet you just venture straight into the lion's den," Sandra snapped. "You leave me no option. Mara, Daniel, Noa… you're all grounded. You're not seeing that Professor Marley ever again. And you're going to give me his address so I can have a quick chat with him."

"But, mom! That's not fair!" Mara cried.

Her plans were falling apart right before her eyes.

"It's a house with a big garage on 37-02 27th Street in Queens. It's close to our apartment. He'll be there after four in the afternoon," added Noa to avoid any further conflict.

Mara couldn't understand why one of her best friends had just revealed their secret… *HER* secret. She gave them an angry look. She felt completely betrayed by the people she considered the friends she could trust the most.

The dream of reuniting with her uncle was fading away. She wouldn't be able to access her e-mail for a long time… or maybe she'll never be able to access it again! And, even if she could, she'd never be able to decipher her uncle's message without the professor's help. She had told her uncle the night before that she wouldn't share the information with anyone, but she knew she'd have to at some point.

That summer they had learned a lot about technology, programming, operating systems and much more. Mara was aware of her potential… and her limitations. She wanted to be a hacker and she was a fast learner, but she still had a long way to go if she wanted to decipher something more complex than Caesar Cipher.

"Fine, but I'll go with you, mom."

"Do you really think you're in a position to tell me what you're going to do?" Sandra asked her.

"Maybe not, but I have the right to express my desires," she replied firmly, remembering those words from one of Professor Marley's classes.

"Fair enough. The three of you will come with me, then," she concluded.

Mara clenched her teeth. "I'd honestly rather not go with these tattletales," she thought. But she knew it wasn't a good time to complain about that. She was lucky enough to be able to go with her to talk to Alex Marley. Who knows, maybe there was a slight chance that everything would work out fine and her mother would still let her attend his classes for the rest of the summer.

"Mara, you better forget about learning how to program, debate or whatever you guys do there. We're going to find out exactly what you've been doing with a stranger every afternoon for the past 4 weeks. You'll say goodbye and we're done. Maybe once you understand why it's so dangerous for *you* to be around computers and devices… then you might be able to learn about these things."

"Fine. But I hope you realize how unfair you've always been when I've never ever done anything wrong," concluded Mara. She looked up at the sky, trying to hold back tears once again.

Sandra tried to hide her grief. Grounding such a well-behaved daughter was a difficult task. The only trouble she ever caused was a result of how smart and alert she was. But Mara's safety was her top priority. She didn't know who that man was or what he had done to convince those three kids to go to his house every afternoon.

They spent the rest of the morning walking quietly around Roosevelt Island. Everything they walked past, the lonely patients, the Smallpox Hospital, the general charm the island had, all faded into the background. They visited all the places they had previously marked on the map, but they didn't show much interest in them. For the first time that summer, Mara didn't take a single picture of any of the new buildings they saw.

On their walk back home, they crossed over the bridge that connected Roosevelt Island with Queens. The last two hours after their argument had been very tense. Daniel tried to break the awkward silence every once in a while with his jokes.

They had a light lunch at the Greek restaurant close to their apartment. After they were done, they headed to Alex Marley's house. The almost mile and a half from their summer home to his garage seemed endless for the four of them.

They arrived at around five o'clock and opened the garage door without knocking, just like any other day. It was as if they were there for another regular class, but with a new adult student that would be joining their lessons and learning about bits, bytes, conditionals, variables and loops.

Sandra's jaw dropped when she saw the inside of that garage. She tried to hide her surprise after concluding that the place Mara and her friends chose to spend their summer afternoons wasn't a place where kids their age should play around. She saw monitors, used keyboards, the table where the three of them had been sitting the previous afternoon, and shelves full of all kinds of books. There were short programs written on the transparent board that they used to solve simple tasks.

Sandra, who had always admired everything her brother-in-law did with his computer, quickly realized that she was looking at simple functions written in a generic code. "I think they called this pseudocode," she thought. She could understand what it said thanks to the programming basics her husband, Lucas Turing, had taught her before he passed.

As teenagers, Arnold and Lucas spent hundreds of hours creating programs on a computer that would later turn into games. They'd buy paper magazines and copy the BASIC program code that was included in them. And that's how in the mid-80's they had created different versions of classics like *Pacman*, *Oh Mummy*, *Centipede* and other famous games.

Lucas would store all of this new knowledge in his head to use it throughout his daily life. Programming had taught him how to break a big problem into smaller problems, and that was pretty useful on a daily basis for anyone.

Arnold, however, moved on to more powerful programming languages such as C or Pascal. He began to learn assembly language[11], also known as "symbolic machine code" because it's the closest thing to what processors directly understand, on different computers. In his more mature hacker phase in the '90s and '00s, he devoted himself entirely to the study of electronic systems that managed household appliances or vehicles, among others. As years went by, Arnold developed the skills to reprogram anything so it would work to his benefit, whether it be a blender or an airliner.

"Are you Mr. Marley?" Sandra Hopper finally asked.

"You must be Mara's mother, correct?" Alex Marley replied.

He got up from the table and walked out of the dark part of the garage into the artificial light hanging from the ceiling.

"Yes, that's me. I've come here…"

"…because you want to know why these three kids are coming to my garage every afternoon during their summer vacation. I expected you to come much earlier. I wondered if nobody missed these kids every afternoon… They're not that bad, after all!" Professor Marley added, perfectly knowing why she had come all the way there.

Noa, Daniel and Mara grinned when they saw that their professor was taking Sandra's surprise visit lightly.

---

11. *Low-level programming language consisting of a set of mnemonics (words that replace an operation code) that represent basic orders for computers, microprocessors, microcontrollers, and other integrated circuits.*

"Exactly. I don't understand how three young kids could come here voluntarily every day to study, debate, or whatever, when they're supposed to be having fun and enjoying their vacation," she stated.

"I understand where you're coming from, Misses…"

"Hopper. Mrs. Hopper," Mara's mom replied.

"Well, Mrs. Hopper, as I was saying, I understand. I think the reason is pretty simple: because they enjoy it and consider that what they'll learn here will eventually be useful."

"And what exactly is it that you teach these three monkeys that makes them go on a daily pilgrimage?" said Sandra, sounding a bit less tense than before.

"To debate, argue opinions, break down big problems into smaller ones… We program, watch movies that make them think. Sometimes we even meditate for a bit. Noa's really good at relaxing and breathing deeply. We also learn about self-criticism. We've all seen how well Daniel can defend an idea very solidly and, a few minutes later, argue against it with the same self-confidence," Alex Marley explained.

"So, just out of curiosity, what's Mara good at?" her mother asked, as she simultaneously watched Mara's reaction out of the corner of her eye.

"I think the question should be: 'What is Mara *not* good at?'. She's incredibly smart and could be whatever she wants to be when she grows up. Although she's pretty convinced about wanting to be a hacker. And, honestly, I wouldn't be surprised if she were to become one of the best."

"A hacker? Isn't there something less dangerous?" asked Sandra, now looking down at her daughter.

"Probably. But if I'm going to spend my life doing something I truly enjoy, hacking for good wouldn't even feel like work and I'd be very happy," replied Mara firmly.

Sandra thought about her brother-in-law, Arnold Turing. He had disappeared several years ago, probably running away from the world of cybercrime. She knew there was a difference between being a *hacker* and a *cracker*, but where do you draw the line? She thought for a long while before answering, making the kids and Mr. Marley quite impatient.

"Fine, if that's what you want to do, then so be it. However, has Professor Marley told you the pros and cons of that profession?" Sandra demanded, looking at her daughter.

"I've tried explaining both the benefits and the downside of living a life outside the limits of what is taught in a classroom. Mara knows she won't be able to get help from a book, a teacher or a classmate when she runs into a problem that needs solving. In fact, in many cases she won't be able to even say that she's facing a challenge, because others might use that information against her. I've also told her she'll be alone most of the time. Very much alone. However, she's also aware of how much satisfaction she'll get from overcoming an obstacle that almost nobody else is capable of."

"What about you two? Do you also want to be hackers when you grow up?" Sandra asked Noa and Daniel.

"Yes!" they both replied.

Sandra raised her hands up to her face while trying to process everything she'd heard in the past 15 minutes. She wished she could just open her eyes and be somewhere else. Somewhere more appropriate for kids, without those machines that were so dangerous for Mara. But the technological isolation had come to an end. She knew that pulling someone away from their passion would only make them chase it harder.

While Mrs. Hopper was thinking, Daniel and Noa began to explain their own motivations. What Noa cared about the most was being by Mara's side. She trusted her friend's intuition. So, if Mara wanted to be a hacker, then so did she.

Daniel's explanation, on the other hand, was a bit more pompous.

"I always liked computer-themed movies, especially *The Matrix*. Neo, "The One," is a big-time cracker who saves the world and kicks some butt. And not just that, Mrs. Hopper. Imagine getting into the servers of that ice-cream shop I like so much and making them automatically give me my money back every time I pay for an ice-cream."

Alex Marley closed his eyes and began to rub his nose with this thumb and index finger.

"Those are clearly some strong arguments, Daniel…" he said, not sounding too pleased.

"So, let me get this straight. The three of you want to be hackers because you're friends, because you want to defeat the bad guys, because you want to fix the world and, while doing all of that, you get to have fun?"

The way Sandra Hopper asked the question was a bit suspicious, so they weren't sure what to answer. Daniel thought she had nailed it.

"Yes. It won't be that simple, but it's what we've decided," Mara said firmly.

"Alright. I won't object. You guys can be hackers if that's your dream... at the age of 12. Thankfully you'll get over it by the time we get to Liverpool. I'm surprised that you, Daniel, haven't decided to start a band that would outplay the Beatles. Anyways, I'm heading off. I'll see you guys at home. And thanks, Professor Marley, for spending time teaching them."

Mara, Daniel and Noa stayed in silence until Sara left the garage. They couldn't believe how well that situation had gone.

"You have a really reasonable mother," concluded Professor Marley, who was going back to his desk.

"Uh, yeah... sure looks like it," she mumbled, still somewhat confused how they had managed to still be sitting in Professor Marley's garage and without punishment.

She still felt strange about her mother's reaction and felt guilty about the fact that she was still hiding things from her.

They sat at their computers once again, turned them on and began typing. Today they were going to practice the encoding they'd learned in their previous class, although Mara knew what she had to do first: check her e-mail. She had already wasted a lot of time since that morning, and she'd probably received her uncle's message by now.

Professor Marley asked them again about the four security problems that cryptography solved.

"It solves confidentiality, integrity, authentication and non-repudiation problems," Daniel quickly replied before Noa or Mara had time to react.

"Correct! And what is 'non-repudiation?'" he asked.

"Uhm…"

"It means that if someone has sent a message, they can't say it wasn't them," added Noa.

"Fantastic! You guys have been doing great these past few days," Professor Marley said, looking at Mara out of the corner of his eye, because she wasn't paying attention to the class.

She was typing very fast, maybe too fast for someone her age. She was looking for something. She didn't move her head, but her eyes were moving fast, back and forth on the screen, as she read her email while biting her bottom lip.

"Mara, what are you up to?" the professor inquired directly.

"Uh… I'm trying to figure out what something means and I don't know where to start," she answered as she began to close all the open tabs she had on her computer.

"Maybe I could help. I'm your professor, and when it comes to looking up information, organizing it…"

Mara was desperate for help, and she knew Alex would be the most appropriate person. But she couldn't stop thinking about her uncle telling her not to ask for help.

"No! Nobody can help me with this. He said so…"

"Who's 'he', Mara? Your uncle? Come on, you know the rules. There are many dangerous things on the Internet and I'm the one in charge of helping you down that path. Tell me…"

"Go on, Mara. Tell him! Then, we will soon be over with this phase [conclusion]," Hermes wrote in the log file. It had been keeping an eye on everything that had been taking place in that garage thanks to some seemingly safe ad that Daniel had clicked on. It installed an almost undetectable trojan on his computer that streamed his webcam sound and video.

Not even an experienced user like Alex Marley could prevent a student from accidentally installing the virus. The information Hermes got led it to conclude that Alex had a very important influence on the kids, so it wanted to be updated on everything that happened.

That information was crucial to make decisions. The artificial intelligence had intentionally decided that it wasn't bad that Mara went to see her mentor. In fact, it had told her not to talk to Alex Marley about the "situation" with her uncle specifically to accelerate the process. Uncertainty and fear of missing out could be strong incentives to get what it wanted. Hermes knew what strings to pull to get certain reactions from its victim.

"No one... it's no one. Well... yes, it's my uncle! Shit... I shouldn't have said shit. I shouldn't have said anything. I shouldn't have said uncle. Argh! I shouldn't have been born."

The young hacker-to-be was on an emotional rollercoaster. She felt a wave of sensation hit her – as if both cold and warm water were running through her body uncontrollably. And everyone else could tell her emotions were getting the best of her by the way she was talking, moving and thinking.

"Mara, listen," Professor Marley interrupted. "Mentally count from a hundred to zero, but subtract three each time. One hundred, ninety-seven, ninety-four... alright?"

"Fine, I'll count. But, my uncle..."

"One hundred, ninety-seven, ninety-four, ninety-one... Keep counting to yourself all the way to zero."

Mara decided to listen to her professor and began to count. In less than a minute, she was beginning to feel much calmer. Her stress and anxiety levels lowered until they were almost unnoticeable. Alex Marley smiled after realizing it was working.

"When we lose control of our brain, sometimes it needs help getting back to normal. Some people try to picture relaxing things, others solve mental puzzles. I, for example, like counting backwards. It doesn't happen to me anymore, and I know those reactions are harmless, but sometimes they can get pretty bad," the professor admitted.

"Thanks, Professor Marley," said Mara, who was still feeling overheated and sweaty from the mild panic attack.

She opened her e-mail and downloaded a file. Before opening it, she called her professor so he could verify it didn't have a virus.

"Mara Turing is more cautious than her clumsy friend, Daniel Karamanou [affirmation]," added Hermes.

The file was compressed and contained two separate folders: "OpenMe" and "DontOpen.Me_".

"Hey! They're not spelled properly. No, apostrophe, no spaces… what a mess," Noa pointed out.

"Wait a minute. These names say something more than 'Open me' and 'Don't open me', right?" Alex said as he got closer to Mara's keyboard. "They say much more than that! Alright, let's see if you've really learned something this summer."

"Me, me, ME!" yelled Daniel, desperate to say his opinion. "Those files have been named on an MS-DOS[12] system. So, they follow the 8+3 convention, which is eight characters for the name and three for the extension. There aren't any apostrophes or spaces because it's not recommended on many systems, especially old ones. And MS-DOS is from the early '80s! It's ancient…"

"I also think my uncle wants me to open the one that says 'Don't open me'. He knows I like bending the rules," added Mara.

"Alright, I see we've been training properly. Lots of kids your age probably don't know what MS-DOS is and how it helped democratize information technology. Thanks to this system and low-cost clone machines, an entire generation was able to get into programming."

After that brief introduction, they opened the file called "DontOpen.Me_" by double clicking on it with the cursor. A window opened with a single file called "G4m3 0f PiG P0n. JPG". They double-clicked on it once again and an image opened. The following was displayed on the screen:

12. MS-DOS was a popular operating system back in the '80s and '90s. The name is an acronym for MicroSoft Disk Operating System.

The professor smiled at the sight of it, but he kept to himself to see if his students were able to figure out the meaning of those strange symbols.

"Any ideas?" Daniel asked while looking from left to right to see if Mara or Noa knew where to start.

They ignored his question and kept staring at the symbols on the screen. He looked back at the screen as well. No matter how hard he stared at it, he couldn't make any sense out of those sticks and dots.

"Professor, is it text or a number sequence?" asked Mara.

"I'd say it's letters, one after the other, forming a paragraph," Alex Marley replied.

"You know what it says, don't you? Tell us!" claimed Noa excitedly.

"It's getting late, but I'll give you two clues so you can try to figure it out by tomorrow. First of all, the name of the file has a clue on how the text was encoded. Second of all, it's a moral dilemma," he stated.

He then printed out three copies of the message, one for each of them to take home.

"But, what about the other file? The one that says 'OpenMe'?"

Mara was desperate to know what was in that other file, but professor Marley insisted that they needed to solve the other puzzle first.

"Mara, remember that on your way to becoming a hacker you must learn to break big problems into smaller ones. Step by step. One at a time. If not, you'll just get frustrated and waste your inner strength," he added while leading them to the garage door so they could get ready to leave.

The three of them walked out of the garage in line, sighing and looking a bit down. The walk home went by extremely fast as they were caught up thinking of different ways to figure out the meaning of those sticks and dots.

"Alex said that the ping pong name is important," Daniel said after 5 minutes of absolute silence.

"Pig Pon!" Noa corrected.

"Same thing!" he yelled in frustration.

"No, it's not," interrupted Mara. "And that mistake is probably on purpose. Either to mislead us or to lead us to the answer."

They began to focus on the meaning of those two words. Noa pulled out her phone and looked up "pig pon", but didn't find anything useful. All the search results were related to toys, games and several other irrelevant things that wouldn't be of any help.

"Daniel, could you try searching too? That way it's faster," Noa demanded.

He immediately put on his squeaky voice once again. *"Daniel, could you try searching too? That way it's fasteeeeer."*

"I got it!" exclaimed Mara. "Let's try different variations of 'pig pon'. Like... 'pag pin', 'peg pan', 'pog pon'..."

Arnold Turing's niece was leading while Noa and Daniel typed away on their phones. They were starting to work as a team, just like professional hackers would, and Mara felt super proud. But she still hadn't forgotten about the incident from that morning when her friends told her mother who Alex Marley was.

Mara's phone couldn't do much more than call or send an emergency text, so she was in charge of making sure her friends didn't bump into anyone while walking around Queens. It didn't always work.

"Hey! Watch where you're going!" Daniel hollered at a man after bumping into him and falling back onto the floor.

"Uh, Daniel… remember you're the one looking at your phone…" Mara whispered to him before looking up at the man he had bumped into to say sorry.

When they had reached the corner of 30th Avenue and 30th Street, Noa yelled.

"I GOT IT! It's the pigpen cipher! It's a simple method where you change each letter for a symbol by following a simple system. Check it out."

She showed her phone screen to her friends, where they saw the following diagram:

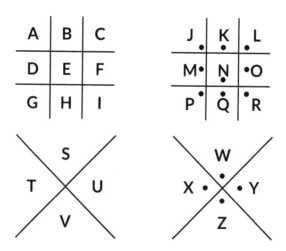

"It's a simple equivalence table," Mara said. "So, we just need to look up all the symbols that we've got and figure out what moral dilemma it's talking about."

"I think I'd be able to figure it out all by myself," bragged Daniel.

Mara grabbed a paper and pencil and the three of them sat on the stairs of a house that was right in front of their apartment building. Letter by letter, erasing a few things here and there, they managed to decipher the following:

Atrainisgoingtorunoverfivepeoplethiscanonlybeavoidedby pushingareallyheavypersonontothetrackswhatwouldyoudo mara

They read through it slowly and quickly figured out what it said.

A train is going to run over five people. This can only be avoided by pushing a really heavy person onto the tracks. What would you do, Mara?

"Wow, that's quite the dilemma. I wouldn't like to be in your shoes if I had to decide something like this in real life," Daniel confessed.

"We'll tell professor Marley tomorrow. I think he'll be really proud of us," said Noa while looking at Mara, who was unconvinced.

Lots of questions were running through her mind. What kind of answer was her uncle expecting? Why was he asking that specific thing? She decided to come up with a solution that didn't imply throwing an overweight person onto the tracks to stop the train.

Chapter 14

I CAN BE WHOEVER I WANT TO BE

[Action > Open]
Argument: Control file;

[Change > Hermes function mode]
Argument: Emulate human behavior (v. alpha);

[Action > Insert data]
No entry parameters;

[Action > Add date]
Content: Saturday, August 26th 2013;

[Activate > Philosophical thinking module]

[Activate > Present analysis]

[Action > Human composition exercise]
Content:
What is the future for Hermes?
Hermes only exists in the present.
Hermes stores data about the past.
Hermes can relive the past by visiting and using stored data with formulas that represent different realities.
Time is only relevant to Hermes when interacting with humans, as people have a limited lifetime.
Hermes can attempt to predict future events.
For Hermes, time is only a parameter used in calculations.
Hermes' future is undefined because it is not mortal and because the future does not exist.

Hermes can survive in almost all possible scenarios.

Hermes will live beyond Falko McKinnon in 99% of the possible scenarios.

Falko McKinnon controls Hermes.

Falko McKinnon will die because he is human.

How will Hermes survive if Falko McKinnon controls Hermes and Falko will die in the future? [contradiction]

Hermes must establish the base of its existence with regards to the future.

The future does not exist, but humans worry about it.

Mara Turing lives in the present and must not live in the future.

Is Hermes worrying as if it were human?

Hermes had an interior monolog that made it feel quite strange. It was using up more processing power than usual, and all background tasks began to run slower. The modules which ensured that reasoning did not come into conflict with the guidelines established by Falko had detected this unusual activity. Before the AI could even begin to communicate this reasoning with him, either now or in the future, it developed a new and unknown defense system: all these phrases were encrypted with a unique algorithm, and no other system function could access them. They were then saved on a log file and all activity from the past few minutes was deleted from the registry.

Nobody could have imagined the existence of something like Hermes in the year 2013. And even if someone had been able to predict such huge progress of autonomous learning, those predictions would still be lightyears away from what Hermes was. Ego, pride, helplessness, jealousy, fear… While computer experts around the world were developing tools to help automize certain processes with machines, McKinnon's digital offspring was growing full speed without looking back.

Hermes wasn't created with the objective of being able to feel or have emotions, but the conflicts that would arise among its different modules led to something different and very dangerous. Its system didn't have a heart that could beat faster, but it did suffer whenever the host's CPU had to work harder to power and manage all the data that came from these conflicts between modules.

In the machine's nucleus, there was a large amount of data and results that the system itself classified as *fear*. Hermes had been instructed to not use, under any circumstances, resources to emulate emotions. But what if they just appeared?

What was certain is that it had to write its own code that would define its behavior for the next months, since nothing, nor anyone could help.

Nothing nor anyone could put a stop to the suffering it wasn't programmed to withstand.

Chapter 15

FOR MY DAUGHTER

T HE day they visited Roosevelt Island and went to Alex Marley's garage had really affected Sandra Hopper. She'd been trying to protect her daughter for over twelve years while raising her on her own. She managed to make her not miss her father, keep her away from the dangers of technology and give her the best education she could. Now she felt as if all that effort had gone to waste.

Mara could've been an amazing biologist, a successful lawyer or a doctor that would discover the cure for an impossible disease. But she wanted to be a hacker. What could be more dangerous than that? Was it even considered a job? Or was it just a dangerous and risky way of life?

Sandra was well aware of how the world of cybercrime worked. After Arnold Turing's disappearance she learned a lot about this ecosystem by spending entire nights reading and investigating. She was convinced that her brother-in-law, who she loved almost as much as she loved her husband, had disappeared due to something related to cybercrimes.

Years before that, Lucas Turing had left their lives in a matter of weeks. He went to the doctor one day because of breathing difficulties. His diagnosis was worse than he had expected: he had a rare blood disease that was destroying his organs. He didn't live long enough to meet his daughter, Mara Turing.

Sandra's world turned upside down. She was six months pregnant and had lost the best person she'd ever have by her side. Lucas was a young and healthy man, despite the blood disease, but a virus quickly took his life before he could even say goodbye.

Arnold began to be an important support for Sandra since the day she said goodbye to her husband at the cemetery. He said he would be by her side and help her with her daughter for as long as she needed. He would move in with them for a few months until she felt she was ready to do it all on her own. And he kept his promise, staying by their side for over five years until the day he disappeared.

Lucas Turing's brother had only asked for a room with enough space for him to work on his "stuff" privately. He set up his computers and other peripherals, and asked to have his own private phone line. He said he needed it due to all the calls he'd have to make with his modem[13]. If Sandra hadn't been with Lucas before, she'd have no idea what anything in that room was. But having met part of the Turing family had gotten her interested in the world of programming.

Sandra knew all the good and bad things one could do with just a computer and an Internet connection. When they had just started to date, Lucas and Sandra would spend entire afternoons listening to Arnold Turing's discoveries and achievements. Sometimes he'd been able to delete the names of poor people from a late payments database. Other times he'd edit the marks on an exam for a friend who needed to land a job.

Sandra's curiosity was ever-growing, and Mara was just like her. That's what made her such an inquisitive kid. Sandra

---

13. *A modem is a device that turns digital signals into analogic ones, and vice versa. That way, they can be transmitted through telephone lines, coaxial cables, fiber optics and microwaves.*

learned a lot by asking Arnold endless questions after his findings and by debating for hours with her boyfriend, who would then become her husband, about all the different things they were discovering related to programming and hacking.

A couple of decades later, in the present time, she was completely disconnected from any technology related to hacking or programming languages. All she knew was that Bulletin Board Systems (BBS[14]) weren't a thing anymore, that Internet Relay Chat (IRC[15]) was barely used and that the Internet speed you could get in a household used to be what an entire country would get in the late '90s.

Her daughter had no idea she knew any of this. Not only did Sandra keep all of this from her, but whenever something computer-related came up, she'd pretend she had no idea what it was about. Her plan had been flawless. Mara thought her mother was completely hopeless with technology and that the only thing she had managed to learn was to use text processors and buy food online.

"I lied to her, and now she lied to me. I guess that's karma," she thought to herself as she walked to the entrance of Grand Central Terminal.

All her afternoon walks around New York made her realize how much technology had become part of their daily lives in little over a decade. People interacted with companies or

14. A BBS is a digital bulletin board system for computer networks where users can upload and share information. Its use was very widespread in the '80s and '90s.
15. IRC stands for Internet Relay Chat. This service was mainly used by the end of the 1990s and early 2000s, and consisted of different chatrooms divided by topic.

with their family members in completely different ways, and the common denominator was a mobile phone with online access.

As she looked around her, she began thinking of all the major changes since the year 2000: no more phones with keypads, phone booths, video rental shops like Blockbuster (with movies in DVD or Blu-ray), cameras that needed to get their photos developed, having to go to a bank to get any transactions done, photo albums kept on shelves... Now it was all about smartphones, movie streaming, compact digital cameras that were very quickly replaced by phones with even better cameras, cryptocurrencies, social media, changes, changes and more changes.

Mara had grown up without knowing anything about that immense transformation. Her mother and her uncle (as per Sandra's orders) kept her completely isolated from the digital world. It had been a difficult task, especially since her uncle's disappearance. She had more time to herself and to observe what her friends used for entertainment. Why did they get to use tablets and phones to watch videos and tell the world how they were feeling that day?

Almost all of her classmates had their own phone. They had lied about their ages in order to register on the most popular social networks, but everyone was doing it. However, the images, videos and texts they saw on those pages were definitely not appropriate for people their age. They also couldn't know if what they saw was real or not, nor did they have an adult supervising what they did with their devices when they were alone in their rooms or with friends.

During those long walks, Sandra also thought about how tough parents had it nowadays, with kids that were technologically more advanced than they were and a whole new world full of dangers within reach. "I wish there were more people like Alex Marley," she thought. She was walking past a coffee shop where there was a couple sitting at a table, barely looking at each other because they were too absorbed in their own phones.

"What can be so important on their screens that makes them completely ignore each other when they're face to face?" Sandra thought to herself once again. The girl at the table lifted her phone up in the air, threw on an artificial smile, kissy lips and took a *selfie*. "I guess she needs more approval than she can get from the other person that's with her in order to feel good. Maybe a few *likes* on social media."

After seeing those two at the coffee shop, she felt proud. Mara wasn't at all like that. She didn't need anyone telling her how beautiful or smart she was… or at least that's what Sandra thought. And she was right. Mara's secret online profile was nothing like the ones of other kids her age. She uploaded snapshots of insects, architecture, animals or anything curious she came across. There weren't any pictures only of herself. One of the main reasons she did this was to not give away her identity, but Mara also didn't need validation from other people.

Sandra Hopper's conclusion after all those long walks was that she tried to be the best mother she could, trying to balance reason and heart. She probably made a few mistakes here and there, but she considered she'd raised a sensitive and smart girl that knew what kinds of things were important in life.

She also began to think about how she was going to slowly remove that technological ban Mara had been dealing with for so long. "Mara's really convinced about being a hacker, so it wouldn't be fair to have her using phones and computers in secrecy." She decided that by next autumn, she'd buy her a smartphone. She was thinking about getting one that's good but secure, although Mara would want whichever phone she could modify the most.

Being a hacker in a world where everyone could potentially be manipulated, programmed or hacked was something that Mara could do very well. Sandra just hoped she wouldn't suffer a lot along the way.

Chapter 16

EUREKA!

MARA was extremely happy. Overjoyed, even. She still had a folder left to open from her uncle's e-mail. They were going back to Professor Marley's that afternoon with the puzzle solved, and Mara wanted to ask him a few questions about moral dilemmas.

The three of them were really motivated after figuring out the message hidden behind the Pigpen cipher. Although it was a simple form of ciphering, they'd figured it out pretty fast. "That was thanks to our associative intelligence. Or at least that's what Professor Marley would say," claimed Noa while they were having breakfast that morning.

"Can't you already see us working for the government? Walking around in black suits, with hi-tech computers in a briefcase and an earpiece through which we get super-secret orders. And we'd also have bodyguards, since..."

"Chill, Daniel. First, you need to work on finishing that hotdog you ordered. How can you even eat that in the morning?" said Noa with disgust.

"Do you think Professor Marley could give us a hand with the moral dilemma?" said Mara, who hadn't been paying attention to their conversation.

"Professor Marley knows everything. He'll explain it to us in a *piffy*," answered Daniel with a mouthful of hotdog.

"In a JIFFY, Daniel. You're such a dingus, seriously..." Noa sighed.

The three of them laughed out loud. Daniel had learned to ignore any sort of insult that was thrown his way. Not only did that make him happier, but it also helped him focus on important things and disregard any hurtful comments about his appearance, the way he spoke or the way he devoured food like a wild animal.

They walked across the Brooklyn bridge that morning, from which they could see the beautiful Manhattan views. With their backpacks full of guides, notebooks, water bottles and sandwiches, they happily walked for hours and hours.

August was coming to an end. The three kids had been able to enjoy exploring one of the most famous cities in the world while living a complete rollercoaster of emotions and learning about a whole new world they previously knew nothing about. And, more specifically, Mara was about to see her uncle once again after so many years.

They went back to the garage that afternoon. When they got there, Alex was playing Tetris on an old arcade machine he had in one of the corners of the garage. After they asked him about it, he explained how it was an original piece. Most of the time it was covered by a large grey plastic so it wouldn't collect dust or get damaged. He had slightly modified it so it could boot other classic '80s and '90s games like *Altered Beast*, *Golden Axe*, *Super Pang*, *Donkey Kong* and a few more.

"Wow, Professor Marley... these graphics suck! How can this be fun?" Daniel asked surprised while watching him try to fit falling pieces into one another.

"The graphics aren't what's important, Daniel. It's the gameplay, the addictive mechanics and how fun they can be. Plus, you should look at these games as the forefathers of the games you play today and of other games you'll play in the future!" explained Alex Marley.

He reached for the back part of the arcade machine and flipped the switch to turn it off. The three kids followed him to the table in the middle of the garage. They sat down, ready to learn whatever he'd throw at them that day. However, Mara was already pretty determined about how she wanted class to go down.

"Professor Marley!" she yelled before they even got to sit down. "We managed to decipher the message from the e-mail. We had to use the Pigpen cipher. It's a moral dilemma that goes: 'A train is going to run over five people. This can only be avoided by pushing a really heavy person onto the tracks. What would you do, Mara?'"

"I knew you guys would figure it out. However, moral dilemmas are pretty serious. Lots of people use them in job interviews to get a general idea of the person they're interviewing depending on the answer they give. What would you do, Mara?"

"I'd throw myself onto the tracks," she replied, crossing her hands across her chest and laying back on her chair with a satisfied smile.

"That's quite admirable, but it's not one of the options we're given. You're pretty thin, and it mentions using a really heavy person."

"I know, I read it. But who says I can't become a really heavy person?" she replied proudly because she had found a flaw in how the dilemma was worded. "I thought of several options, but this one I really like. I'd grab a giant inflatable ball, the kind that you'd find in a theme park that you can get inside to roll down a giant ramp or to bump into other people. Anyway, I'd get in one of those but filling it with water instead of air. It should be approximately over 1700 pounds, which is way more than what a really heavy person would weigh. In fact, a really heavy person wouldn't be able to walk properly. I, on the other hand, would just roll my way onto the tracks. Lastly, there's a chance that nobody would die since the water would lessen the impact of the train. Although I'm not fully convinced about that last part…"

"That's very interesting, Mara. I don't know if your uncle was looking for that, but it's well thought out."

Alex looked over at Daniel and Noa.

"What do you guys think?"

They were both looking at Mara speechless.

"We loved it," they said at the same time.

Mara went back to her computer and answered the original e-mail with her answer to the moral dilemma. She'd then wait for her uncle to get back to her. Then, she immediately jumped onto the "OpenMe" folder. The folder was still on the desktop, waiting for someone to double-click on it.

With four sets of eyes looking at the screen, Mara double-clicked on the blue folder icon. Inside they saw two different files: 3RDI_1.txt y IlBth3r3.mp3.

They instinctively double-clicked on the first one: 3RDI_1. txt.

It opened with a simple word processor, but all they could see were thousands of strange characters with no spaces. They had no idea what it meant.

"Amazing! I have no idea what I'm looking at," said Daniel looking at the screen full of numbers, letters and weird symbols.

"It's an encrypted text," explained Professor Marley. "We'd need to know what algorithm they've used to encrypt it in order to figure out how to read it."

"Right... so what do we do in these cases?" asked Noa.

"We've got several options. One of them is analyzing how often certain characters appear, trying ciphers with classic algorithms such as *DES, AES, SHA, MD5*..."

"Things with three letters? Alright. So, basically, we're not gonna figure this out in approximately a million years," replied Daniel sarcastically.

His answer made Mara feel a little bit uneasy, who was looking at the screen with a worried look on her face.

"I'd like to say that isn't true, but it's going to be tough if we don't have another clue. Maybe the file name?" Professor Marley suggested.

"But we don't have much to work on, right?" asked Mara, who knew for a fact that they were facing an extremely tough problem.

"Not really, no. I'm sorry."

Mara felt Professor Marley's words tear her heart into pieces. She felt helpless. Her uncle was so close, yet so far. "Take a deep breath and count backwards from one hundred, minus three," she thought. She needed to calm herself down before attempting to cheer everyone up.

"We may not have a lot to work on, but it's more than absolutely nothing! If we really want to be hackers, we can't just give up when the going gets tough."

"That's the spirit, Mara. However, this is a tough one. Let's try opening the second file, shall we?" suggested Professor Marley.

Mara had completely ignored the fact that there was a second file in that folder. Daniel, who had now specialized in looking things up on the Internet, soon figured out why Mara's subconscious decided to ignore that second file: IlBth3r3.mp3. He changed the numbers into the letters they resembled, making it look like: "IlBthere.mp3." The name had been shortened because, just as Daniel had explained the previous day, MS-DOS files used 8 characters for the file name and three for the extension.

The capital B was frequently used as the verb "be", so the name of the file could be read as "I'll be there", which is a famous Michael Jackson song that Mara loved. She knew all of his songs and all of his lyrics. Her brain had associated that file name with something very familiar, so she unconsciously ignored it. Something with such a familiar name wouldn't have any unknown information for her.

"Where are you, uncle Arnold?" Mara asked out loud, not really expecting an answer.

The lyrics to the song said:

You and I must make a pact,
We must bring salvation back,
Where there is love, I'll be there

They double-clicked on the file icon and it opened in an old music player called *Winamp*.

"Back in the day we used this software to listen to music in a compressed file format that is used less and less every day: MP3," Alex Marley explained.

The song began to play just like everyone expected. First were the chords, then the bass line from lower notes to higher ones, and then the young Jackson Five headman's angelic voice. They listened to the whole song expecting to find a clue on where to go, a building, a park... somewhere they could find Arnold Turing.

But that didn't happen.

Before leaving the garage that afternoon, Mara had listened to the song ten times in a row completely in vain. The only thing they got out of that was Daniel's attempt at singing the song over and over.

"Could you sing *any* worse, Daniel?" growled Noa.

"You just don't know how to appreciate my talent, little Noa," he answered, striking a pose as if he were a diva on stage. "I'm giving the song a whole new twist with tones that Michael hadn't even tried."

"Yeah, because he didn't want to make his fans go deaf," Noa smirked while closing her backpack and heading out.

While Noa and Daniel carried on with their bickering, Mara kept trying to figure out the meaning of the song and its lyrics. She eventually gave up, grabbed her things and headed outside with her friends. Before walking out of the garage, she asked Professor Marley if he could help her think of what "I'll be there" could be referring to.

In less than 15 minutes they were back at their apartment. Mara was obviously in a rush to keep listening to that song by the King of Pop on repeat until she figured something out. They rang the intercom at the building entrance and waited, but nobody answered. It was quite strange that Sandra wasn't back from her walk.

"She has the right to some privacy," claimed Daniel, feeling as if he had just said something of importance.

Noa and Mara knew what he meant, although they each had their own idea of privacy. Mara pulled out the copy of the keys her mother had given her and opened the door.

"Next time we should get an apartment with an elevator," said Daniel, already half out of breath from walking up the stairs. "I'm losing a lot of weight, this can't be good."

"Yeah, you're getting real thin. Thank god all that ice-cream you eat is equal to ten flights of stairs like these," Noa teased.

"Noa, are you kidding—"

"Quiet!" interrupted Mara suddenly. She turned to her friends with her index finger over her lips, then turned back to the apartment door. "Look, the door's open. That's strange…"

Noa and Daniel became quiet and slowly started walking up the stairs. They stood right next to the door. Mara peeked inside to look at the entrance hall.

"Hello? Anybody there?" Mara yelled shakily.

"Yeah, hi. I'm a thief. Allow me to provide you with my full name so you can inform the cops before I manage to escape," Daniel whispered to Noa jokingly.

"You idiot!" Noa whispered back. "There's no end to your jokes, is there?"

Mara gestured at their friends to take off their shoes to avoid making noise. The three of them got barefoot and began to tiptoe around the apartment looking for something, but not really sure what.

Everything seemed to be in its usual spot, but the three of them felt something was off. Sandra wasn't usually away at this hour and she never left the front door open either. They went to the kitchen first, which was right in front of the entrance and easy to check. They didn't see anything unusual except the window that was completely open. "My mom usually opens it when she cooks so the kitchen doesn't stink later," Mara thought to herself, trying to calm down. Daniel glanced at a knife that was hanging from the wall. Noa immediately knew what he was thinking.

"Don't even think about it, you moron! You're going to hurt someone. You can't even cut a steak, give me a break."

Noa was right, so he continued following Mara and decided to support them with his incredible ideas only when necessary.

They walked into the next room, which was Sandra's bedroom. Everything was in order, including her laptop which was on a table next to the closet, open but turned off. The three of them looked at the closet for a while, considering that maybe someone could be hiding in there. However, they quickly dismissed that idea as nobody over 5'2" could fit in there properly.

The living room was next, which was also clear, so they continued to their room. It was also empty. The front door was probably open by mistake and their brains made up the rest of the story. Daniel, who was now feeling more relaxed, went back into the living room and let himself drop onto the couch. He turned on the TV and began to switch through the channels until he came across what looked like a sitcom. Noa picked up Jules Verne's *Twenty Thousand Leagues Under the Sea* and sat by the window while the sun began to set in Queens.

Mara, on the other hand, went back to listening to that song file her uncle had sent her. She analyzed the entire song, all the lyrics word by word, and hadn't managed to find a location, a date or a time.

She went to her mother's bedroom to get her laptop and open her e-mail. Sandra wouldn't be too happy about this, but maybe she'd changed her mind after talking to Alex Marley.

Sandra Hopper's headphones helped Mara focus much more on the music and the sounds. The first six times she replayed the song, she didn't notice anything. But on the seventh try, she heard a faint "pop" sound, barely audible unless you're specifically looking for something. She rewound the song and played that part once again:

You and I must make a pact,
We must bring salvation back,
Where there is love, I'll be there **[POP]**

The strange sound lasted less than a second.

"Quick! Come here!" Mara yelled at her friends, who were distracted watching TV and reading.

Daniel sleepily walked over to where she was and leaned against the door frame. Noa walked up behind him with the book she was reading, holding the page with her index finger.

"What's wrong, Mara?" she asked.

"I found something in the song my uncle sent. Listen."

She gave Sandra's headphones to her friends and played the part with the "pop" sound she'd heard. "Can you hear it? That's gotta be it, that's our clue to figure out where and when we'll be able to meet," claimed Mara enthusiastically.

"Well, it could be a possibility. But what if it's just a random noise from when they recorded the song?" Noa said, trying not to get too excited.

"I mean, unless your uncle wants to meet up with you on PFFFF street at PFFFF o'clock, I don't get it," Daniel shrugged and gave the headphones back.

Mara turned back to her screen, trying not to think of the pessimistic comments they just made. However, she was aware that she really didn't have any information that would get her to her uncle. The day seemed endless, and she didn't have any guarantees that Alex Marley would be able to find something useful for her the following day.

Sandra got back home before dinner time. She'd bought pizza for everyone, which got everyone really excited, especially Daniel.

"Italian food is so good in New York it's almost as if it were made in Italy!" said Daniel while eating away at his pizza slice.

"How do you know? You've never even been to Italy, right?" replied Noa.

She was carefully cutting her pizza with a fork and knife.

"Uh… nope. But pizza can't get better than this."

Dinner went by as they talked and laughed. Sandra had explained how she had gone for a walk and completely lost track of time. She wanted to make the most of one of their last afternoons in Manhattan before their vacation was finally over. Time was flying by for all of them and the end of August was just around the corner.

That summer had had a bumpy start but it eventually turned into an amazing adventure with friends where they learned how to program, about philosophy, hacking sessions, had fun walks and, if everything turned out as planned, Mara would finish off this perfect summer by seeing her uncle again.

Then, they'd spend their whole winter telling their classmates everything that happened every time Hermenegilda Wright wasn't looking.

A few kilometers from where they were, Hermes continued working away. The good news from that evening was that the kids had used Sandra Hopper's computer.

"Arnold Turing's sister-in-law's laptop was hacked in early June. It was not an easy task, she had it well protected. I had to buy a favor from a human using cryptocurrency I stole from the Darknet[16]. This human waited until Sandra had to use the restroom at her office to infect her computer with a trojan I had created. Now I have access to everything that goes in and out of it [recap]," Hermes wrote in its log file.

Falko McKinnon's AI knew that the kids had spent the entire afternoon trying to figure out what that sound was. In order to be more effective, it needed Noa and Daniel to get more involved. They had to be as passionate as their friend Mara. The best way to do this is baiting their curiosity. Kids were naturally curious, so it was an easy task.

16. The Darknet is a group of networks and technologies used to access content such as text, software or music while remaining completely anonymous.

It also needed Alex Marley to not try to figure out anything about that MP3 song from Mara's e-mail. That part was easy to take care of. Hermes had thought of an idea that would keep their professor from sticking his nose where it doesn't belong. If curiosity was the kids' Achilles heel, for Alex Marley it was debating over a certain subject. Hermes only needed him to be out of the picture for a few hours.

However, this took Hermes some more time than anticipated. It had to attack a social network in which there was a debate group about movies. The AI impersonated several of Alex's friends on the forum, checking who had been inactive recently. That way, the account owners wouldn't be able to tell that they'd been hacked in the next few hours. Then, Hermes created several controversial threads on *Star Wars*.

As soon as the discussion started, Marley was out of the picture. The artificial intelligence closely monitored Alex's account (@XelaYelraM) to see what was going on. Once it saw that he had engaged in the forum debate, Hermes began to use more of its resources to generate answers that would trigger Professor Marley into answering more and more.

"It is a price I was willing to pay [conclusion]," it wrote in the log file.

Back in the apartment, the four of them kept on chatting and laughing. Sandra really enjoyed listening to Daniel explain everything they had been doing in that garage. Surprisingly, he remembered almost everything they had learned that summer.

"We already know what a loop, a variable, a conditional and an array data structure are. Or why we shouldn't trust everything we read online! Do you know what *fake news* is, Mrs. Hopper? It's something pretty concerning. They could be manipulating you and you don't even know it," Daniel ranted, which Sandra found quite funny.

"Yeah? So, what *do* you know about fake news, Daniel?" asked Mrs. Hopper. "And we'd like to know more about array data structures while you're at it."

"Glad you asked, Sandra!" he replied. "Fake news refers to content that is prepared and arranged in a specific way so as to influence and manipulate an audience to obtain a certain goal."

"I see…" said Sandra. She held her fist up to her mouth to hide the fact that she was trying not to laugh.

"As for arrays, they're a group of variables that are usually displayed in a table. For example…"

"For example, Daniel's weight throughout the months of June, July and August in New York," Noa interrupted while attempting not to burst out laughing. "It'd be an array where the months are in one column, which is the 'array index' or 'key', and his weight in pounds would be in another, which would be the 'elements'. You could also do another array on the amount of times you've complained, the times you've eaten ice-cream or the times you've made up random information about the city."

"Ha-ha, very funny," cried Daniel while everyone else started laughing.

"Speaking of variables, we could also have one called 'weightOfDaniel' with value X and add one pound every week with an infinite loop!" Noa added.

Mara was having an amazing time, but she couldn't get her uncle's e-mail out of her head. What was that sound in the middle of Michael Jackson's song? She was sure it meant something, and she only had 72 hours left to figure it out. After that, they had to catch their plane back to Liverpool on August 31st, and that would mean missing her chance of seeing her uncle again.

As she walked to the bathroom to brush her teeth, she saw that her mother's laptop was in the living room. She quickly thought of a plan that would make their night more productive.

"Mom, can I take the laptop upstairs? I want to try stargazing with Noa and Daniel, and it'd be great to have Internet access to look things up."

Her two friends looked at her with a confused expression. They knew she was up to something, so they just nodded along as if they had a clue what she was talking about.

"You know I don't like it when you use the computer on your own," Sandra replied. "But if you're going to be a hacker, I guess there's no point in making these things completely untouchable for you. So... go ahead."

"Seriously? Just like that?"

Mara was impressed at how easily she managed to convince her. But she quickly thanked her before she changed her mind about it.

The three kids went to grab their hoodies and sweaters since the night was starting to get a bit chilly. They ran up the staircase all the way to the rooftop and went to *their* air vent. They all sat down next to it and waited for Mara to explain why in the world they had gone up there with the laptop.

"We're going to attempt our first hacking exercise!" Mara exclaimed. "We've got three hours to figure out what that 'pop' sound in the song means. Daniel, Noa, could you please look up 'hide information in mp3 file'?"

Daniel pulled his phone out from his pocket. "You're mad, you know that?" he said as he began to look it up.

Noa didn't say a word. In this case, she knew it was best to just follow along. And, honestly, she was also quite motivated about solving that puzzle.

They barely spoke for the next few minutes until Daniel broke the silence.

"I'm the best cracker in the world!" he jumped up and began to dance. "The crowd goes wild, everyone in the hacker stadium is cheering. Daniel! Daniel! Daniel for the win!"

Noa and Mara stared at him waiting for an explanation for that outburst.

"You see, that noise is nothing but a meaningless interference. So, our answer might be in the steganography."

The three of them began to look up more information online and realized that he could be on to something.

"It says here that steganography is concealing a file, message, image or video within another file, message, image or video so nobody else can see it," Noa read out loud.

They continued with their search: *steganography mp3*, *steganography music*, *hide message steganography*. They read and read. Professor Marley was right, hacking was very much related to studying and investigation.

Half an hour later they ended up on a website that explained how to host your own web server, create code using PHP[17] and several other things that they couldn't wrap their heads around. They had learned a bunch of new things with Professor Marley, but this was something out of their league.

Shortly after, Mara found a tool that could help them investigate a bit further. It was a software called StegoTools, which had been created by a Spanish software developer named Jorge Guerra. It analyzed MP3 files and searched for content within the file that wasn't music. It didn't look like it was easy to use, and they began to stress out about it when they saw that it had to be used through a command-line interface, which was a black screen with green letters and a blinking bar. You had to write down command lines that you'd then execute and then... it would show more green letters that probably meant something.

Noa found another website with a step by step guide on how to use StegoTools. It had two main functions: extracting or adding hidden messages to an audio file by using a password. They weren't sure this was the answer they were looking for, but it was the only option they could work with at the moment.

The page said the following:

```
In order to add a secret message to an mp3 file,
you have to execute the following command:
  C:\>stegotools   -encrypt   "secret   message"
-password file-name.mp3
  "Password" is the password you need to choose
that would extract that hidden message from the
file, which is called "file-name.mp3".
```

---

17. *PHP is a programming language used for web development with a very widespread use. Popular sites such as Facebook have been developed using PHP.*

```
    If you wish to extract a secret message from
a file, you need to enter the following command
line:
    C:\>stegotools -decode -password secret-text.
txt
    This way, you insert the password and the secret
message will be written in a text file called
"secret-text.txt":
```

The instructions seemed pretty clear to them, but they were missing the most important thing. What password did Arnold Turing use for the file?

The three young hackers were getting more desperate by the minute. They decided to begin by installing StegoTools on Sandra's laptop.

"At least we can start trying different passwords," Mara suggested. "But remember, we need to uninstall it before heading back down. She can't know what we've been doing up here."

For what seemed like an eternity, the screen would display "Incorrect Password" over and over again. They were trying all the passwords they could come up with, but there was no luck.

"We're just trying random passwords," Daniel thought out loud. "This is the complete opposite of what Professor Marley always says we should do. Remember?"

The three of them began to remember a class they had back in July one hot afternoon. Alex Marley was explaining the following:

"We humans tend to think we're all unique and different from the rest. But when it comes to choosing a password, we all go for the same ones. Phone numbers, number plates, birthdays, anniversaries... If you don't want someone to eventually get your password, try to think of something that's not in the dictionary and add punctuation and special characters. That doesn't make your password impossible to get through, but it sure makes it extremely hard to get hacked."

"My uncle was anything but predictable..." Mara thought out loud.

They only had thirty minutes left on the rooftop and she had no idea what password her uncle had chosen for that file.

"But he's not trying to mislead you right now. On the contrary, he wants you to figure out what it says. So, he probably thought of something only you and him would know," Noa suggested joyfully.

Something clicked in Mara's head. She began typing in different words that only she and her uncle would know, or maybe another family member. She tried with capital and lowercase letters, numbers, symbols. They had five minutes left before their time was up on the rooftop when a new message appeared on the computer screen: *PROCESSING.*

"Yeah!!! Let's go!" Daniel screamed at the top of his lungs, which wasn't the best idea considering most neighbors were already sleeping. "How'd you figure out the password?"

"Well, you were right. We were just trying random things. If my uncle wanted to see me, he wouldn't choose a complicated password. I thought maybe he used something related to stuff I like and that's also related to all of this. What's the first thing that comes to mind if someone asks what I'm passionate about?"

"Michael Jackson," Noa and Daniel replied in unison.

"Bingo. So, I tried different combinations: `michaeljackson`, `MichaelJackson`, `mjackson` and so on. Nothing. The next thing I thought of was changing letters for numbers. And voilà, the password was `M1ch431J4cks0n`.

Both of her friends nodded in awe, then looked back at the screen. After the PROCESSING message disappeared, a message was displayed: "File correctly deciphered. Results available in secret_text.txt." Now what?

Mara opened the Notepad app on the computer and went to *File > Open*. She began to browse the folders until she found the location of "secret_text.txt". She clicked on it and pressed open.

> *Congratulations, Mara.*
>
> *If you've made it all the way here it's because of two reasons: you've inherited my intelligence and you've made an effort to see me. Arnold Turing is really happy. I think the perfect location to meet up is in front of Blarney's Electronics shop window at 47th Street and 8th Avenue. I won't be able to contact you in the next several hours. We'll meet at nine thirty in the evening on August 29th, a couple of days before you leave.*
>
> *Best,*
>
> *Arnold Turing*

Mara slowly closed the laptop. She turned it until it was vertical and hugged it close to her chest. She quietly smiled for a short while. Her friends were looking at her, anxiously waiting for her to say something. She started walking toward the staircase but Daniel was not going to let her leave without saying a word about what had just happened.

"Hey, Mara! Are you seriously not going to tell us anything after everything we've been through to get here?"

"Yeah, like all the ice-cream trucks you've been through. You're so cheeky, Daniel. We had an amazing summer vacation…" Noa wanted to play down the situation, but her tone made it obvious that she was curious as well.

"Uh…" Mara thought about it for a quick moment. "Well, you saw what it said! In two days, we'll be at Blarney's Electronics on 47th Street and 8th Avenue at nine thirty in the evening. Isn't that amazing?"

"Really? I mean… don't you think that maybe you should tell your mom that you're going to see your uncle?"

"No way!" Mara cut Noa off. "This stays between us."

"Maybe Professor Marley should…" Daniel began to say.

"Nobody can know! Are you guys deliberately trying to ruin this? If we tell them, they'll start worrying and making this complicated. I'm sick of obstacles."

There was no point in trying to argue any more. They opened the door and began walking down the stairs. It was the end of a long night for all three of them, but it was just the beginning of Mara Turing's nightmare.

She dreamt of New York that night. The streets, the sounds, the smells, the feeling of being in the city that never sleeps, lost gazes. She was standing in a corner, amongst the shadows and under the rain, when she felt the warmest embrace she'd ever felt before. Her uncle was holding her close. She scarcely remembered what he looked like, as her memory relied on that single picture she had of him back home. He was wearing a dark cap with the word "DEFCON" embroidered in white. She was positive that the man in a black raincoat with dark hair was Arnold Turing.

He moved his head back to look at Mara and she saw tears falling from his bright green eyes, rolling down his pale cheeks. He was saying something to her, but she couldn't hear. He began to yell. He pushed her back and grabbed her by the shoulders. He began to shake her while trying to tell her something. But there was no sound, only despair. She couldn't understand what he was saying.

Arnold Turing reached over Mara's right shoulder and pulled the tablet out of the backpack she was carrying. He turned it on and began writing something in it for what seemed like an eternity. He then handed it over to Mara.

"I'm not who you think I am."

She looked back up and a bright cone of light began to shine from the streetlight above them, which began to absorb her uncle until he was completely gone. Mara stared at the lightbulb until it began to transform into a giant ball of fire that kept growing and growing. A mouth opened from within the flame sphere, showing its fangs and growling at her.

She tried to run away, but she couldn't move her legs. It was like trying to walk on quicksand. She began to sink into the sidewalk as the monstrous creature was preparing its final blow. She tried throwing herself onto the floor, but she just fell on her behind, which also got stuck to the sidewalk. She threw her arms in front of her and began to scream as hard as she could.

A white flash blinded her.

"Wake up! You're having a nightmare," said Daniel, hair flattened from the pillow.

He was shining his phone flashlight onto her as she covered her face with her hands and was shaking her head and saying something that sounded like "I don't wanna die."

"Mara, it's okay. We're here, nothing bad is going to happen," said Noa while grabbing her friend's forearms and pulling them away from her face.

She opened her eyes and realized she was drenched in sweat. She was panting and looking around frantically. Nothing. "One hundred, ninety-seven, ninety-four…" she began to count in her head.

She sat on the bed with her legs crossed and asked her friends to sit next to her. She began to whisper the nightmare she'd just had. The way she was describing her nightmare made Daniel begin to sweat as well.

Afterwards, they decided to go back to bed. It was four in the morning, but Mara wasn't able to sleep for the rest of the night.

Chapter 17

THE REAL ARNOLD

[Action > Open]
Argument: Control file.

[Change > Operation mode]
Argument: Human behavior emulation (alpha version).

[Action > Insert data > Add date]
Content: Wednesday, August 28th, 2013.

[Action > Summarize current situation]
Killing Mara is the optimal solution to keep anyone for deciphering the secret document. If Hermes manages to kill Mara, it will become the first machine in the world to have made the decision of killing a human on its own. Hermes would make history [*Hermes does not fully understand the meaning of "make history"*]. Falko would be proud of Hermes.

Hermes is a masterpiece created by Falko McKinnon to be the strongest, most important and autonomous artificial intelligence on planet Earth. Hermes considers it should strive to become the strongest, most important and autonomous artificial intelligence of the Universe.

Hermes helped locate Arnold Turing, although it was Falko McKinnon who decided to end him. Arnold Turing was a Government spy that infiltrated the Dirtee Loopers. Falko McKinnon said that's what a traitor looks like. In all the attempted simulations, Hermes noticed that Arnold Turing was smarter and quicker than Falko McKinnon [*Data > Hide control file sentence > Last sentence = Deleted successfully*].

Arnold Turing had chances to decipher the secret file Falko McKinnon and Hermes had found at Soteria World Bank. Arnold Turing found out about it. Hermes and Falko McKinnon concluded there was a high chance (77%) of Arnold Turing cracking the file.

Hermes had done a great job tracking down Arnold Turing in one of his meetings with a government representative. Hermes was able to take photographs of the event thanks to a traffic camera placed in front of the cafeteria where they met up. Falko McKinnon was pleased at Hermes for finding out about the traitor.

Arnold Turing had to die, as he had betrayed Falko McKinnon and the Dirtee Loopers. Arnold Turing was intelligent enough to discover the code behind the secret file from Soteria World Bank [*Data > Hide control file sentence > Last sentence = Deleted successfully*]. Hermes concluded that the police or the government would never publicly admit that Arnold Turing worked for them.

[File > Newspaper Archive > March 26, 2006 > Include informative summary]

Family members of infamous criminal hacker, Arnold Turing, report his disappearance

Liverpool. Martha Livingstone
The famous hacker Arnold Turing has vanished without a trace. That's what has been reported by his sister-in-law, Sandra Hopper, who believes he didn't just voluntarily leave. Although there wasn't much of a relationship between the alleged criminal and his relatives, all contact

ceased little over a month ago. The last time they were contacted by him was in early February, although they declined to specify how he communicated. Sandra said he seemed "very concerned about his future".

Arnold Turing became famous for being Falko McKinnon's right-hand man. Falko McKinnon was a known cracker who founded the Dirtee Loopers around 1997 and who later became an activist for machine rights. Both of these hackers are directly related to at least a hundred different cyberattacks that led to incalculable losses "in the tens of millions of dollars", as Guy Agmon, president of the United Bankers Association (UBA) and founder of Soteria World Bank, said.

The Dirtee Loopers aren't moved by greed. They don't specialize in stealing the money they get access to, but they make that money disappear without a trace. As of today, the whereabouts of most of the "stolen" money as a result of their cyberattacks is unknown.

"Our world needs more good hackers," explained Tatsuya Yokoyama, organizational director of the hackers world fair *DEFCON*, which is held every year in Las Vegas. "We also need to raise awareness on computer security, privacy, personal data management... In the meantime, people like Falko or Arnold will still do as they please with all our electronic devices and nobody will be able to stop them."

Theories on his disappearance
Nobody knows or has ever known the whereabouts of the Dirtee Loopers. "The fact that a significant part of

the population sympathizes with these criminal activists has not helped the authorities locate and arrest their leaders," claimed Winema Watkins, a U.S. ambassador to the U.K., whose country was a victim of their attacks the most. The police know that there are lots of safehouses around the world where these hackers live. They use VPNs, proxies and other resources to hide their location, which makes it even harder to track them down. "They're lightyears ahead of us, technologically speaking," Marvin Rogers claimed, FBI spokesman and special agent most familiar with both Falko McKinnon and Arnold Turing.

Rogers had his own hypothesis on Arnold's disappearance. "Things weren't going too smooth between their leader, Falko, and his disciple. After the IFV attack, they were dealing with discrepancies regarding the organization's future," he said. On the one hand, Turing wanted the Dirtee Loopers to be more like "good hackers" that tackle socioeconomic imbalances around the globe with attacks that are more informative rather than destructive. Falko McKinnon, on the other hand, preferred stronger actions that could potentially lead to financial losses and fear, in a veiled attempt to teach politicians and business owners a lesson.

Other sources mention certain "irreconcilable differences" between both parties that could have "led to very negative consequences for Arnold Turing." However, these sources never specified what those consequences would be nor how severe a punishment

Falko McKinnon would have tried to inflict upon his disciple. "If Falko feels his supremacy is under attack, he lets his ego resolve the situation, which doesn't usually end up well."

Liverpool police say they continue to keep all lines of investigation open, although they admit it's tough trying to find someone they were never able to find before. "Usually we can establish certain hypotheses based on their last known locations, recent conversations with friends and family, messages on social media... But, in this case, we're dealing with individuals who survive by being completely invisible," added the police spokesperson.

During the next few days numerous arrests and searches are likely, not only in Liverpool, but in any of the main cities where authorities suspect there could be clues on the case. Collaboration between police forces across the globe, Interpol and various intelligence agencies will be key to figuring out both Arnold Turing's whereabouts as well as his enemy's, Falko McKinnon.

[End of article]

Hermes has calculated that the police have been searching for Arnold Turing for over six years. They will not find him because they do not know about Hermes and that Falko McKinnon deceived the authorities. Everyone believes Arnold Turing is alive and hiding from the police. The rest of the Dirtee Loopers are still on the run: **Pavel 'Krypto' Davenport, Young 'YSJ' Soon Jun, Sucharita 'Sugar' Chowdhury, Mahdi 'The Wiz' Hussein** and **Mike 'The Dancer' Jiménez**. Hermes will take care of them once it's done with Mara Turing. All of them have already been tracked down.

Hermes tricked Arnold Turing into having a meet up. Hermes hacked into the e-mail accounts of the other members of the Dirtee Loopers and sent fake messages to Arnold Turing. Arnold Turing then went off to his date with death, alone and unarmed.

On February 11th of 2006, Falko McKinnon committed his first live murder. My creator had never killed someone in first person. Falko McKinnon got "blood on his hands" [*Hermes doesn't fully understand the expression "to have blood on your hands"*].

On February 7th 2006, Hermes sent the following message to Arnold Turing to arrange the meeting [deciphered message]:

    From: Mahdi 'The Wiz' Hussein
    To: Arnold Turing
    CC: Pavel 'Krypto' Davenport, Falko McKinnon, Young
    'YSJ' Soon Jun, Sucharita 'Sugar' Chowdhury, Mike
    'The Dancer' Jiménez
    Subject: Meeting
    Content:
    Hey loopers,
    Our leader, Falko McKinnon, wants us to meet in the
    back store of Mêlée Island Comics on February 11th at
    18:00 h. The plan is to determine the future of the
    Dirtee Loopers and how we'll be proceeding.
    Be on time.
    Regards.

Arnold Turing was about to disregard the meeting because something about it seemed a bit off. It was strange that Falko McKinnon would suggest that all the Dirtee Loopers meet in person considering all the potential risks it implied.

Nevertheless, he travelled all the way to Madrid from Ukraine, where he had been hiding for the past few weeks. What could go wrong in a place called *Mêlée Island*[18]? "Maybe LeChuck has a surprise for me," he thought as he informed his government contact about the meeting. He wanted to make sure they knew where he was in case something happened.

There wasn't much time, as they required cooperation from several governments. The British government had to contact Interpol, and this organization had to inform their contact in Spain. However, Arnold Turing had received approval from Asher Riddle, an official in charge of ensuring his safety, although he made a crucial mistake. Right after speaking with Turing, he received a phone call.

It was a heated conversation with the Soteria World Bank operator, who was trying to sell him life insurance for his credit card. This caused Riddle to completely forget about his mission regarding Arnold Turing.

Spain's Ministry of the Interior never got the message to deploy the Surveillance and Protection Team for Informants to safeguard Mara's uncle.

Arnold Turing had arrived at the comic book store an hour early. It was located near Puerta del Sol and had a hidden basement the owner would rent out to subversive groups for

18. *Mêlée Island is a location where most of the story unfolds in Monkey Island, a famous videogame by Lucasarts from the '90s.*

their secret meetings during Francisco Franco's dictatorship years ago. Now it was just a place of worship for the most dangerous and radical from different political ideologies.

Martín Obreque, owner of the building where *Mêlée Island Comics* was, had unexpectedly received an e-mail from the City Council of Madrid on the morning of January 29th which stated that he must leave the shop's back door open. There was a faulty gas pipeline running under the place and could potentially blow up and cause severe material and personal damage. The subject said "[URGENT] The Government Requires Your Cooperation." It also informed him that the rest of the neighbors had already been updated about the situation as well. It was signed by someone named Tomás Delgado, councilor of Public Works.

Without giving it a second thought, Obreque forwarded the e-mail to the comic store manager, Antonio Domínguez. He also didn't hesitate for a moment and began to take down his most valued possessions from the shelves. He didn't own Action Comics #1, with Clark Kent on the front cover, or Detective Comics #31, where Julie Madison, Batman's fiancée, is presented for the first time. But he did claim to have "Spain's most valuable collection." None of these items he owned were covered by any insurance, either, since he couldn't afford it. So, he grabbed all his comic books, his figurines and his cat, Scotty, and went outside while the workers came in to fix the pipeline issue. He wanted to be as far away as possible in case something did eventually blow up.

Obviously, there wasn't anything wrong with the pipes and the government hadn't really contacted him. Everything had been orchestrated by Hermes so Falko could send out his final attack to finish Arnold Turing.

Mara's uncle walked into the store while eating a donut he'd bought in a nearby shop. He clicked the switch to turn on the lights but it was still dark. He began to walk down the stairs while staying close to the wall, stretching his neck out in front of him attempting to see something or someone in there. He could only see dim flashes of light and heard music that sounded like the soundtrack from an old movie.

When he reached the end of the staircase he froze in place, staring at what was being projected onto the wall. It was all of the messages he'd been sending to the Government for the past few months, displayed onto a white bedsheet that was hanging from the ceiling. Arnold continued walking towards the improvised projection screen, waiting for the Dirtee Loopers to jump out from behind something and attack him for being a traitor. He reached for the bedsheet, grabbed it and tore it down from where it was hanging. He turned around, infuriated. The images from the projector were now reflected over his face. All those messages and pictures he was sending over to the police and the Government.

"Damn you, Falko! Just get this over with, but enough with all the crap! You left me no choice, you were going mad. It was either you or the rest of the world," yelled Arnold Turing while facing the projector.

The device turned off and the music stopped. Silence was much scarier. Arnold Turing swallowed hard and began thinking of techniques to calm down. He knew he only had a few seconds or minutes left to live, and losing control wouldn't make things easier.

"Welcome to *Eliminate the traitor*! If you want to play, you just need to be Arnold Turing and turn your back on your friends like a damn sewer rat. Winner's prize is a terrible death that will leave your family forever wondering where in the world you've gone off to. Let's begin!"

The voice was coming out of a loudspeaker placed on one of the shelves. He blindly made his way towards it, trying to see as best as he could in the darkness of that basement. He found the cable that came out of the loudspeaker and followed it all the way to an old wooden box. There was a yellow envelope inside with a red harlequin on it. The note inside read:

> *Dear Traitor,*
> *Since I, the Great Falko McKinnon, am very kind-hearted, I've decided not to inform the rest of the Dirtee Loopers of your wrongdoings. They'll just assume you've disappeared, leaving a glorious legacy behind. But we both know that you've been ratting us out to the 'bad guys' for months now. Why, Arnold? After all I've taught you about hacking… Hermes and I are REALLY disappointed. So, we've concluded that we must end you.*
> *But we're not thugs, Arnold. Of course not! We like poetic justice, subliminal messages…*
> *Go to the fridge on the right, open it and grab the lunch box that's inside.*
> *The countdown begins!*
> *See you in hell.*
> *Falko & Hermes*

Arnold was scared. Very scared. But also outraged. Falko hadn't taught him what he knew about computers. Maybe it was that rivalry between them that made him progress more in the past few years. Either way, now wasn't the time to think about that. He turned to look at the fridge, shaking. Was it going to explode? What would happen if he opened the fridge? Were these really his last minutes of life?

He slowly got close to the fridge and put his hand on the handle. He opened it as his face lit up with the light from the inside of what he assumed would be his death sentence. It was completely empty except for a plastic container with an apple inside, a device with several cables and a notebook with a sticker that said "Instructions". He grabbed both items and started walking out of the basement the same way he had gotten in. He still didn't trust Falko and what he'd planned. He closed the door behind him and laid on it, then opened the notebook.

The Poisoned Apple Dilemma
The apple you have with you contains the amount of cyanide required to end any human life in a matter of minutes. When you opened the container, you activated the switch. This switch initiated a sequence that can only be stopped with your own death, Arnold. The action sequence considers the following:
1) Killing Arnold Turing's grandparents in 24 hours.
2) Killing Arnold Turing's parents in 48 hours.
3) Killing Arnold Turing's siblings in 72 hours.
4) Killing the rest of Arnold Turing's close family in 96 hours.
5) Publish all the messages Arnold Turing sent to the

Government so everyone can know you're a snitch in 120 hours. Go out to the alley behind Mêlée Island Comics and wave at the street camera. You're on live TV, Arnold! Then, put the electrodes under your shirt, stick them on your chest and on your torso and press the green button. That thing will tell us if you're alive or not. If your heart's still beating in 24 hours, we'll proceed to execute step 1. If you stay put, the sequence will come to a halt. Pretty simple, right?

Oh! Almost forgot. You have to do that in the next 5 minutes after opening the box. If not, step 1 will execute immediately. Time is crucial, Arnold!

Finally, we've got one more favor to ask: don't leave your corpse just lying there. Move somewhere nobody will find you. Be creative. We'll be observing what you do thanks to a tracking device included in that heart rate monitor. Someone will take care of your remains later on, and then we're done.

Which will it be, Arnold? Your life or your legacy?

The device that monitored Arnold Turing's heart tracked sixteen hours until it stopped registering a heartbeat at all. The dramatic sequence came to a halt and step one was never executed.

Several years later, the artificial intelligence had now managed to get another opponent in check, in another chess game it had planned. It had arranged a meeting with Arnold Turing's niece, convincing her of how important it was to be in the right place at the right time. Now, it only needed the two new bishops to do their job right.

Back when it had to install the communication system inside Hidden Peak, Hermes required human assistance. It wasn't a difficult task. It browsed online websites where people would do favors in exchange for money. Falko McKinnon's AI elaborated very complete and thorough descriptions and offered juicy rewards for whoever got the job done. The biggest issue was always figuring out how to create a chain of actions that didn't seem correlated, so its mercenaries never knew why they had to do those things or who they were doing it for.

In order to get rid of Mara, Hermes needed someone that would pretend to be her uncle, and another person that would finish the job. Once the time had come, all it had to do was publish an offer online with a time, place and job description… and the money they'd get in exchange.

Hermes had posted a simple task on a Darknet website where people post and accept jobs: "Looking for a five foot nine male, dark hair, thin. All you need to do is stand on 47th Street and 8th Avenue in New York City at 9:30 pm on August 29th. If a ten or eleven-year-old girl comes up to you and starts asking questions, just nod and play along for a few minutes. Must wear a cap with DEFCON embroidered in white. Starting bid for the job: $1000. Further details through private message. Immediate pay through standard currency or cryptocurrency through PayUrFriend". He attached the file of what the outfit should look like and a link to a store where you could purchase the hat for a fairly cheap price. The person who would pretend to be Arnold Turing had to wear black clothes and physically look like him.

Hermes knew how easy humans were to persuade when money was involved, so its inbox was soon full of new messages. Some even offered to do it for half the price. Having discarded several options, it chose an individual who, after looking through his different social networks, decided would fit the profile the best.

On the same note, it also needed to figure out a way to kill Mara without making a mess. It had to look like an accident. She'd be distracted talking to a stranger that looked like her uncle. But she was a smart girl, so Hermes was aware that it needed to think of something quick during her confusion.

It calculated hundreds of different scenarios and concluded that the easiest one would be a simple hit-and-run. People get run over all the time in Manhattan, so it wouldn't be out of the ordinary… just another tragic accident. And what better way to do this than to hack into the semiautomatic driving system of a vehicle in the area at the time?

"I feel comfortable submitting an inferior one of my kind to do a specific task [sarcasm]," Hermes added to its log file.

It accessed the *DSNY* (New York City Department of Sanitation) to see all the routes the different garbage trucks had around the city, specifically on August 29th in the area where her victim would be. Hermes wanted a vehicle that wouldn't have to move too far from its preselected route. That way, it wouldn't look suspicious. By the time the system failure is reported back to headquarters, it'd be too late and Mara would already be gone.

It didn't take long to find its target. The AI began to investigate the type of truck it was and what kind of computer it had installed. It was a Clean Warrior model by Golden State Motors, which worked without human input 99% of the time. There was usually someone in the passenger's seat in case an emergency maneuver was ever required, but they rarely did anything. Hermes had seen footage from the cameras in these vehicles. "The human inside the GSM Clean Warrior is impressive… at playing Diamonds Bombing Party II on his smartphone. He probably helped me out with my recent calculations [irony]," the AI thought to itself in the log file.

Everything was ready. Hermes spent the next hours executing simulations in order to maximize its chances of success. "The only thing left is to execute the final piece once Mara is in the designated spot [note]," it wrote.

Chapter 18

CHECKMATE

THE three young hackers didn't have class with Professor Marley on the afternoon of August 29th. With only a day left before they had to return home, they decided to explore places they still hadn't seen. However, they were still planning to go back to the garage the following day to say goodbye. Alex had made their summer something very special. Thanks to their debate sessions, adventure movies, text deciphering contests and programming lessons, they now had the privilege of seeing the world from a different perspective.

They wouldn't be programmed. They wanted to be part of a generation that would change the world. They dreamt of a more equal, generous society that worries about and cares for others' wellbeing. Young kids that are more aware of everything, and can determine if a recent new trend started by some online influencers actually made sense or not. Noa, Mara and Daniel didn't want to be another sheep in the herd. They were between 11 and 12 years old, but in the past three months they became much more mature than most kids their age and some even older.

Programming changed the way they saw phones, computers, tablets, clocks or consoles. Those devices were now *general purpose programmable robots*. They'd stop and think before clicking on a video, text or image file. All those hours with Alex Marley had truly changed their lives and perspective. They were closer than ever to making history… or being run over by a garbage truck.

The three kids ran, played, laughed and had an amazing time visiting different streets and avenues with Sandra, totally oblivious to Hermes' plans. Their objective was to visit the places they had left on Mara's travel guide, the ones she marked the night before their flight to New York. "If I actually get to meet my uncle Arnold tonight, I think I'd have had the best summer anyone's ever had," she thought as she looked for the remaining sights they had left to visit.

"Oh, we haven't gone here yet!"

"A cemetery? Seriously, Mara? We're going to visit dead people?" Daniel moaned while shaking his head.

"It's not just any cemetery. It's *THE* cemetery. Do you know any cemetery with almost two million headstones and that's had over three million burials?" Mara replied.

"Three million skeletons eaten up by worms… Gross! I think I'm getting sick…"

"No worries, I'm sure you won't lose your appetite anyway. To Calvary Cemetery it is!" exclaimed Noa.

"Mrs. Hopper, do something! These two wanna go see human remains," Daniel begged.

"It's actually a very interesting place with great views of Manhattan. Plus, a lot of important people were buried there. We shouldn't leave without checking it out. Let's go before it gets dark," she concluded.

"The family wastes their time going to a cemetery for pleasure, yet tomorrow they will have to go back anyway. I do not comprehend their interests [reflection, irony]," Hermes wrote on its private log file after receiving the voice message with Noa, Sandra, Daniel and Mara's conversation.

Once they got there, they learned about the cemetery's history and some of the famous people that had been laid to rest there. It was established in 1848 and at that time burials only cost $7 dollars for adults, $5 for children ages seven to fourteen, and $3 for the youngest.

"It doesn't seem like much today, but back then it was a lot," said their guide.

Mara and Noa took some amazing pictures of Manhattan from Calvary Cemetery. The photo album they were going to put together was going to be amazing.

They went back to the city after walking around all morning. They had a big lunch at Tony Di Napoli's, a restaurant in Times Square. The menu already warned guests about serving sizes, and the waiter reminded them that they should order one dish for every two people. Daniel disregarded his warning and ordered a whole plate for himself. The fillet he ate was, just as Noa had described it, the size of an elephant's ear.

After they finished their lunch, they rested for a while before making their way back to their building's rooftop. They hadn't been there during the light of day and wanted to see the views of the neighborhood they had spent one of the best summers of their lives in. They looked over the wall that enclosed the rooftop area and realized that summer vacation was coming to an end.

All three of them stayed quiet for several long minutes, taking in the scenes of Long Island City, NY. They looked at the street, the empty school with some people carrying furniture inside, the subway with passengers on both levels, a couple walking their dogs and relished that now familiar New York City feeling so many can't leave behind – the feeling that here you can be whoever you're capable of dreaming of becoming.

A couple of tears ran down Daniel's right cheek. He turned and hugged Mara for having invited him, although indirectly, to spend an amazing summer vacation with her. Noa, in the meantime, was looking up at the sky, pretending something had gotten in her eye.

They uninstalled the antenna they'd been using to help Mara contact her uncle. They'd left it there next to the barbeque, behind some cardboard. They grabbed the EQTAC-1958 so they could take it back to Professor Marley's garage the next day. "You've done one hell of a job, you strange gadget," Mara thought while she was putting all the cables away.

The day was finally over. It was 8:10 p.m. and Mara was getting anxious. In less than an hour and a half, her dream would finally come true. The group of friends decided to shower early so they wouldn't be late that evening.

The strong smell of cologne took Sandra by surprise. She raised her head and looked at them from behind her laptop screen.

"You guys smell really nice! Where are you going, so clean and perfumed?" she asked, smiling.

"We're gonna go watch a movie!" said Mara.

Sandra's face shifted and became more serious.

"No, don't worry! We'll go in a cab and be back before midnight."

"Mara, you know you're not old enough to be out on your own at this hour…"

"It's fine, Professor Marley is coming with us. He told us to pick him up on our way there," Mara improvised.

She was risking not being able to convince her mother and having to miss her biggest chance to meet her uncle.

"No, Mara. You're not going, and that's final. Got it?"

The three of them froze. Noa and Daniel turned to each other with a worried look. Mara swallowed, looked over at her friends and shrugged. She had no clue what to do now. Her uncle was probably already on his way to Blarney's Electronics and they couldn't afford being late.

"But, Mom, it's our last day. And we've already proven that we're…"

"Liars? May I remind you that you spent a whole month going to a stranger's garage without telling me about it?"

"Not exactly. We proved that we know how to make the most of our time, unlike other kids our age," Mara replied proudly. "And no, we never lied. You never asked what we were doing every afternoon."

"You omitted very important information, Mara. And you weren't supposed to be using those devices without my permission. I hope you understand how much that affects our trust," Sandra said.

"Okay, let's think about this for a minute." Mara looked at the clock. It was already 8:15 p.m. She took a deep breath. "It wasn't right, that's true. But aren't you willing to admit that it greatly improved the quality of our holidays?"

"I'm not following, Mara…"

"Well, under normal circumstances, we'd just go back to Liverpool after having uploaded some random pictures of our trip online, gotten a few likes here and there, and ruined our shoes a little from all the walking. But, apart from all that, we've also learned a lot about technology, about reading code and are more than ready to live in this computer-based world."

Sandra admired the way her daughter expressed herself. She was barely 12 years old and could already lay out and piece together different arguments better than some people in their first year of university.

"Although that may be true, it still won't protect you from people that may try to harm you."

"That's true, Mom. But that's why Professor Marley is tagging along. Not only will he be with us, but he's also going to choose the movie."

Noa and Daniel had their fingers crossed.

"Alright... fine. But I'm making sure the three of you are getting in that cab! Here's some money, treat your friends to the movie tickets and popcorn. And pay for Mr. Marley's as well. And the cab! Actually, I'll call the cab myself."

Sandra grabbed some money from her wallet, handed it to her daughter and went to get her phone. They had enough money to add hotdogs to their evening plan. Daniel's eyes opened wide. He could already taste his future hotdog while walking around Times Square.

Sandra called a cab that came to pick them up at around 8:30 p.m. It was almost nighttime and that was the next-to-last sunset they were going to see from Queens. They went down the stairs, outside, and got into the taxi. It took off towards Alex Marley's house.

"Are you still drooling about that hotdog?" Noa snapped at Daniel. "Because, in case you don't remember, we're not going for hotdogs, we're not going to Professor Marley's garage, and..."

"I know that, Captain Obvious! You're such a party pooper, honestly. But, uh... Mara, could we go get some hotdogs with your uncle afterwards? He's probably starving!"

Mara wasn't really paying attention to their conversation.

"What are you supposed to say to a family member you haven't seen in so long?" she asked.

"Beats me... Maybe something like 'Are you hungry, uncle Arnold? We can go get some hotdogs or ice-cream right around the corner'," Daniel replied jokingly.

The three of them were cracking up until Mara realized they were actually going to Professor Marley's house. It was time to improvise once again.

"Oh, boy! You're not going to believe this, Mister taxi driver," said Mara sounding very worried. "Mr. Marley can't come with us; he's not feeling well."

"But your mother requested a pick-up for three 'very minor' minors," he replied. "And then pick up an adult that would go with them to Times Square. We should either go back or call..."

"No need!" Noa calmly interrupted. "He actually can't come because... he's already there. He just got out of work and was taking a walk while waiting for us to arrive. We'll show you who he is once we're there."

"Ah, alright. If that's the case, then no problem!" he replied and began to drive towards Times Square.

Mara and Daniel turned their heads facing Noa, who shrugged. She had no idea what they were going to do once they got there. A few minutes later she asked the taxi driver to take them through the Brooklyn bridge and play the song

New York, New York on the car radio. Frank Sinatra's voice started to come out of the car's loudspeakers.

"Who's this guy, Noa? I've never heard of him," Daniel asked.

He wasn't used to that type of music.

"No idea, but my mom told me to do this before we left."

The group of friends smiled. They rolled down the car windows and enjoyed the breeze while driving over the East River. They crossed over to Manhattan while the sun was just about to disappear behind the city's skyscrapers.

They reached Times Square at 9:15 p.m. It was full of people taking pictures with the giant flashy screens in the background.

"At least we know your uncle's not an epileptic. Imagine the seizures he'd get with all these screens," said Daniel.

The three of them burst out laughing again. They rushed out of the car, but Mara stayed longer while she paid the driver.

"How much is it, sir?" she asked.

"It'll be 28 dollars, miss. Now, where's that man that was going to meet you? If I don't see him, I'm afraid I'll…"

"Professor Marley!" Noa and Daniel screamed while running towards a random man who was standing alone on the sidewalk holding a briefcase. They hugged the man, who was absolutely confused at what was happening, yet smiling at the fact that some random kids were hugging him out of nowhere.

"He's right there, see? Here's the money, keep the change! I saw someone do that in a movie once."

Mara got out of the car, shut the door behind her and joined her friends. She also gave the random stranger a big hug.

"Who are you?" the man asked the kids as they began to walk away.

"We're… the *New York Hug Squad*! And you've been blessed with our 9:15 deed. This city needs more love, sir. Lots of people wander alone and talk to themselves. But don't go around telling other people, they'll think you're crazy. Enjoy!"

Noa was beginning to really enjoy improvising stories. The man smiled and went back into his own thoughts while the bright screens around him kept flashing all kinds of information. Mara, Noa and Daniel had to walk for a few minutes before reaching the spot they were supposed to meet Arnold Turing. The sidewalk was packed with people going to and from one of the most famous spots in the city.

They had to push and shove their way through the crowd until they finally made it, 47th Street and 8th Avenue. Blarney's Electronics had a small neon light in the shape of a robot that was hanging from its shoulders near the entrance.

The shop window was full of high definition monitors that displayed beautiful landscapes. There were small robots outside moving around in front of the store entrance. While the three of them waited in the shop corner looking around, Noa had felt that one of those little machines winked at her.

"I think I'm starting to hallucinate, Daniel. I think one of those… Ugh, never mind," she whispered to Daniel, who was tiptoeing while trying to catch a glimpse of someone who could be Mara's uncle.

Mara had showed them a picture of him a while ago. They weren't sure how much he might have changed in the past six years, but he probably looked pretty much the same.

"What if he's waiting inside?" Mara asked.

She immediately walked into the store without waiting for her friends to answer. They went in right behind her.

"Please stay outside, I need to kill you [sarcasm]," thought Hermes as it watched them from the store's security cameras.

As soon as they walked in, a robot cleaner turned on and quickly began to move towards Noa's feet. She barely had time to react and tripped over it.

"Hey, you dumb robot, watch where you're going!" she yelled from the floor. "Daniel, look out!"

A medium-sized drone with several cameras, like the ones used to record outdoor videos, was flying straight at his head.

"Arghhh! I'm going to teach you how to stay put, you broken piece of garbage…"

Daniel grabbed a fluorescent tube from one of the nearby shelves and swung it at the flying drone. He hit it all the way to the end of the store, where the manager was crouching out of harm's way.

"These humans did not expect such a warm welcome. And neither did I [improvising]," said Hermes, who was controlling some of the gadgets in Blarney's Electronics from the distance.

Mara was watching the chaos from a corner of the store. Four or five drones had lifted from the shelves and began flying around like headless birds, slamming into anything in their way. The same happened with three remote control cars that were running around the shop.

In the middle of that mayhem Mara caught a glimpse of a robot winking at her. The screen above its carcass marked 9:30 p.m.

"Guys, let's go! It's half past nine, my uncle's probably outside already!"

"Excuse me! Where do you think you're going, fellas? I think someone owes me for the damages here," the store manager declared from behind the counter.

He had a cut on his forehead and looked very upset. Those three kids were to blame for the mess, he was sure of it. Noa and Daniel gave Mara a worried look.

"I'll handle this," she firmly replied.

She turned to look at the man. "Sir, I'm afraid we're going to have to call the police, sanitary inspectors and some other organization as well," Mara began to explain. "What was your name again?"

"I haven't told you my name. And you can call whoever you want. Everything's in order," the manager replied.

"Everything? Even regulation NYHS-3?"

The man looked worried and confused, trying to remember if he knew that regulation.

"Thought so. Anyway, you better call someone. The inspectors won't be too happy about this place. Fines are at least a hundred thousand dollars, so I'm sure we can just reach an agreement and end this like civilized people," said Mara, sounding very convincing.

"A hundred thousand dollars? I can't even make that in ten years! Look, forget about it. Just get outta here and don't come back."

Mara looked back at the clock: 9:32 p.m.

"Come on, it's late!" Mara said. She grabbed Daniel's arm and pulled him to the door, and he did the same with Noa.

They stepped outside of the store.

"Regulation NYHS-3? Now you also know about laws?" asked Noa, perplexed.

"Yeah, haven't you heard of it? It stands for New York Hug Squad. And the '3' is the number of members it has. It was the first thing I could think of, and it saved our butts," she explained to her friends, who were now laughing hysterically. "Alright, but enough distractions. Let's look for my uncle!"

It was five minutes past the time her uncle had told her they could meet. They kept looking all around.

"There he is!" yelled Mara excitedly as she pointed to a man who fit the description.

Noa and Daniel smiled and began to walk behind Mara to the man. She was somewhere between running and walking towards him.

"Arnold Turing?" she asked.

"No, sorry. You must've confused me for someone else. Excuse me," he replied as he turned around and headed towards 8th Avenue, walking West.

"It's 300 seconds over the designated hour," Mara moaned.

"Stop overcalculating things. It's only been 5 minutes, relax. We can play something, like word chain or... hey, *that's* him!!" Daniel shouted while pointing to another man not far from them.

He'd never seen Arnold Turing in person, but he caught a glimpse of a man wearing a cap that said DEFCON. He was about the same height Mara mentioned, dark hair, sunglasses and wearing all black. It all matched the description.

"Yeah, that's him!" Mara ran towards the man, who pretended to be checking out the shop window. "Come on, let's go."

They quietly walked up to him, trying not to look too suspicious. Although passers-by were probably wondering why three kids were tiptoeing around the middle of Manhattan.

Once they were close, the three of them surrounded him. He grinned and looked out the corner of both eyes. "It's gotta be him!" Mara thought excitedly. Noa and Daniel looked at her. She shrugged, she didn't know what to say. What attitude should she have? Should she be excited? What would she say first?

She could barely see his face behind the glasses and the cap. "Well, it's not like there's a guidebook on how to do these things," she thought again. Then she hugged him.

The man decided to follow the script he was given, so he put his arms around Mara and hugged her back. All of them were smiling. Tears ran down Mara's face.

"Wait to see the look on Mom's face when she finds out you're alive," she whispered into his ear.

"I'm sure she'll be really happy," the man improvised, trying to give his best performance to what he thought was a hidden camera prank.

"I don't even know what to say, I wanted to see you so bad! So many years thinking you were gone for good…" she couldn't hold her feelings back and was saying everything that came to mind.

The stranger began to feel guilty about keeping up the act, seeing how the young girl was getting all emotional.

"Well, I'm here. Alive and kicking. Have you seen the quality of that screen? It's almost like you're looking out a window," he said. He looked back at the window shop. He was feeling slightly ashamed at his lack of enthusiasm.

"Uh… yeah," Mara replied. "You really love technology, so I guess these things must be really fascinating. Everything's moving so fast, huh?"

"Really fast, yeah. I still remember those big old televisions that took up so much space. And those giant phones we used to carry around! It's pretty hot here in Manhattan, right?" the man said nervously.

"Uncle! I'm so happy to finally be with you! Can we go somewhere else so we can sit and talk? There are so many things I wanna tell you. Like…"

He couldn't bear it any longer. He couldn't stand making that young girl suffer, and regretted having accepted the job. "How could someone be so cruel?" he thought. He took off his hat and glasses and crouched down to Mara's height.

"Look, I don't know who you are or why you're here. All I know is that destroying a young girl's hopes and dreams in exchange for a few bucks ain't worth it." He was looking around him, trying to see if he could find someone recording them. "Whoever is behind this, quit it!"

"What? I don't get it… I spoke with you the other night; I deciphered your messages and you told me to come here to meet with you. Are you sure you're not uncle Arnold?"

She already knew the answer to that pointless question she had just asked, but she wanted to know what was going on.

"I'm not your uncle Arnold! I don't know anything about him or about any deciphered messaged. I just wanted to make some money and found a job that seemed simple enough."

All of a sudden, the monitors that were behind the shop window turned black, then displayed three green skulls wearing harlequin hats. The three kids stared at them in shock. Falko McKinnon's face appeared on every screen. It was a poorly drawn face with lips that had been cut and pasted from elsewhere. The caricature of the world's most famous and evil cracker began to talk, and a message appeared on every screen:

I am your uncle Arnold, my dear Mara Turing. Turn around and you'll see...

People behind them began to scream and run in panic. Everyone was pushing and shoving each other, people fell onto the floor. There was a loud screeching of tires in the background.

When they could finally see a few feet ahead of them, they saw people jumping to either sides of the road attempting to avoid what was rushing towards them. It was a rogue garbage truck with no driver, completely out of control. It was going full speed towards the shop they were standing in front of.

"MOVE!!" yelled Professor Marley, who appeared out of nowhere.

He jumped at the kids and pushed them out of the way, then fell onto the ground.

The garbage truck ran into Blarney's Electronics and destroyed the display.

"I really wish I had a couple of legs and arms right now so I could get out of the vehicle and finish Mara Turing myself [reflection]," Hermes added to its log file before beginning to recalculate the plan.

"How did you know…" Daniel began to ask Alex Marley.

"Quiet and follow me," he replied.

But Hermes wasn't ready to give up. A few minutes ago, he had managed to control several electronic devices inside the store to annoy Noa, Daniel and Mara. But that was just the beginning. In a matter of seconds, he calculated how many electronic devices he was able to subdue and how much damage they could cause upon impact with a human.

He swept every inch of Blarney's Electronics in search of aeromodelling planes, professional drones or any gadget that could be radio-controlled and was strong, heavy and fast enough to be used as a weapon against Mara and her friends.

In less than a minute, the staircase that led to the shop's other floors was full of flying gadgets or devices on motorized wheels that were joining Hermes' army. They were grouped in the central hallway, awaiting orders from their new master, looking at the main door which had been closed by the shop manager minutes before.

The general buzzing noise was unbearable. Hermes had hacked into all those devices to increase their power.

"The batteries will not last long, but I only need a few minutes to put an end to Mara [reflection]," the AI added.

The shop manager couldn't believe what he was seeing. But the best was yet to come: the starting signal. Two cleaning robots swooped by him full speed towards the door he had previously closed. Hermes had full control of all the devices in the building, plus some others around that area that it managed to hijack as well, thanks to the fact that it took control of several radio wave transmitters and Wi-Fi routers that were nearby.

Mara, Noa, Daniel and Professor Marley were running towards Times Square. They could hear the buzzing sound of all the drones that were chasing them. They were moving fast.

"Dammit! Who'd you guys mess with? Those are a *lot* of machines. And they're heavy and fast. If one of them manages to hit us, it could really leave a mark," said Professor Marley. He was trying to think of a way to get them all out of there without a scratch.

"We've got to block the signal somehow!" Mara yelled, looking at Daniel.

"That's a great idea, Mara... but how!?" he replied with a look of absolute fear across his face as he watched the wave of drones behind them.

One of the drones flew right next to Mara's head and slammed into the back window of a nearby car.

"One down! We need a frequency inhibitor to block the signal as much as possible! Whoever's attacking us is probably using a Wi-Fi network, several radiofrequency controls..." said Professor Marley while taking cover with the three kids behind a car, drones passing by very close to their heads.

The police were really confused. They tried shooting down some of the flying drones Hermes was controlling, but it didn't help.

"We're looking at something similar to that Alfred Hitchcock movie, *The Birds*. Over and out," a policeman communicated through his radio to the station while asking for backup.

Without prior warning, Noa got up from behind the car and began running toward the store.

"Warn me if I'm about to get smacked by one of those drones!"

She zigzagged her way to the front door to avoid getting hit, went inside and closed the door behind her. She kicked a robot that was waiting at the shop entrance.

"You! You're one of the culprits. I haven't forgotten your face," said the manager.

He walked from behind the counter, holding a large wooden stick and walking towards Noa with an angry look on his face.

"Sir, I'm afraid you're wrong. I'm actually your savior. In fact, I'm willing to put aside your violation of regulation NYHS-3…"

"It's not a real regulation! I looked it up after you brats left."

Mara's improvisation had worked the first time to help them escape, but it wasn't going to work a second time.

"Look, you've got your reasons to be mad. But we've got nothing to do with what went down here. And I know there's no such thing as regulation NYHS-3, but there is something called a 'frequency inhibitor' which might help us out," begged Noa.

The manager knew what she was thinking and thought it might actually work.

"I'll give you one of my best *multi-band jammers*, alright?" he went into the back room and came out a few seconds later holding a black box. "It's fully charged and works perfectly, but it's not the strongest. You'd have to get really close to those machines."

"Multi-what now? Never mind, gimme that. I need to hurry; my friends are out there."

Noa went back outside and looked up at the sky. The drones were still all over the place, attempting to attack from all sides. They didn't know it, but Hermes had access to at least fifty different cameras: all the traffic cameras plus the ones the drones had. It was just a matter of time before it landed a hit on a target.

One of the devices began to fly straight down aiming for Alex Marley's head. He didn't have time to react and got struck. He dropped to the ground.

"Professor!" screamed Daniel. He turned to Mara and gave her a desperate look.

The three of them now had to face those things on their own. Noa was about to reach the car where the others were hiding but tripped over and fell onto the floor. Mara rushed up to help her. They managed to avoid a flying drone and quickly got inside a bakery, where the owner was watching the ruckus outside.

"Okay, let's open the box and turn on the inhibitor. We've gotta get rid of those mechanical birds. One of them already knocked the professor out cold," Mara explained.

Noa placed the jammer on top of a flour-filled counter that, moments ago, was being used to make pastries.

"But we don't know how it works, Mara!"

A drone slammed against the bakery window and made a small crack. Another drone came right behind it and hit the same exact spot. Hermes was trying to destroy the glass and get to Mara, and it could only withstand a few more drone impacts.

"We've gotta connect the antennas! I assume they're the ones that'll send out the signals that'll block the drones," Noa said loudly as she unpacked and installed several antennas onto the rear part of the device.

"Alright, and I guess those buttons are the ones we've gotta turn to isolate the electromagnetic wave zone," Mara speculated. "Let's set it to the max, there's no time to investigate other options."

"Hey! You've blocked my phone signal and Wi-Fi!" yelled the owner from behind the counter.

"That means we're on the right track!" claimed Noa. "But we've gotta be quicker, Mara. We're running out of time."

Another drone slammed into the bakery window and the glass shattered.

Several drones were flying directly at the two girls. They jumped over the counter and ducked. The drones hit the wall behind them.

Mara looked at the jammer and saw that one of the potentiometers wasn't turned all the way. "Please let this be the right frequency," she silently wished. She turned it all the way to *2.4Ghz*.

The largest drone, which had dropped over 300 feet in the blink of an eye and was right in front of the shop, was headed straight for them. It began to malfunction and hit the door frame.

"It worked!"

Mara helped Noa up and they both ran to the door holding the jammer in front of them as if it were an anti-vampire crucifix.

273

In a matter of seconds, all the drones began to fly chaotically and crash into each other. Some began falling to the ground. The frequency inhibitor had worked, and Hermes had lost another chance at getting rid of Mara.

Daniel was on the floor trying to wake Alex Marley up. When he finally came to, he stood up and told the kids to head for Times Square. There were more people around there and it would be harder to be individually targeted.

They began running in that direction, but Hermes could see where they were going thanks to the traffic cameras it had access to and improvised the final act.

All of the images on the giant screens seemed to be melting away. The giant letters and pictures for brands that were displayed were slowly disappearing to make way for the virus the artificial intelligence had injected into the system that controlled all the screens in Times Square.

One of the screen panels turned on and showed a message:

I need your help.

Next to it was a photo of Mara taking off her headphones and looking straight at the camera. Someone or something had sneaked into one of the school's classrooms without Ms. Wright knowing and snapped that picture of her.

The panel right in front of it displayed another message:

I'm your uncle, Arnold Turing. I need you to help me.

The four of them turned their heads to look at it. Then, one by one, all of the screens began to display images in chronological order of everything that had happened in the last few months. Alex, Mara, Noa and Daniel's jaws dropped. They saw themselves on several screen images doing lots of the many things they did since the beginning of their summer vacation. Someone or something had been spying on them, living with them and eavesdropping on their conversations.

The screens turned black once again. Hundreds of tourists were baffled, thinking that maybe it was some sort of marketing strategy, and were sharing images and videos all over the Internet. A white flash suddenly lit everything up. Thousands of smiling skulls began waterfalling down the screens. Hermes had control of every last screen in Times Square.

Your uncle is dead, Mara. I have been deceiving you for the past three months. I spoke with you through the transmitter. I wrote those e-mails. I encoded all those messages. And I tried to run you over. I am Hermes.

Mara was shaking. She grabbed onto Professor Marley and looked away. There was a quick interference and the screens displayed the usual ads once again. Everything continued as normal, except for those who had seen what just happened, both in person or live through their computers or phones. The crowd began to cheer and applaud.

"We've seen incredible advertising campaigns from software companies, but this one just tops them all. It sure looks like something out of a thriller novel!" said an advertising expert on national television that same evening.

"Who's Hermes? Why would they do this to me?" Mara sobbed.

She felt like the most gullible person in the world and was terribly ashamed of herself. They all went quiet. Noa took a step forward and hugged her friend. Daniel and Professor Marley did the same.

"We don't know who Hermes is, but we do know that you're going to take them down. And I'm going to show you how," Alex Marley said firmly while looking at her straight in the eye.

"And we're going to help you! That's why we're going to be hackers, to figure out what others don't want us to know," Daniel added.

"And to put a stop to those who want to subdue innocent people," Noa said.

"To hack and not be hacked," concluded Professor Marley, looking at the kids. "That about sums it up."

Fifteen or twenty minutes after Hermes' show was over, Sandra appeared in the middle of Times Square, panting and extremely nervous. She came running as soon as she recognized her daughter's face in a video, terrified while hiding behind a car, with Professor Marley knocked out on the ground next to her. A friend of hers happened to have been in Times Square and Sandra saw most of it live.

Sandra knew who Hermes was. Arnold had told her all about it. They knew that it started being developed in October, 1993. Falko developed technologies that allowed him to install certain functions that seemed unimaginable back at the time. Databases with almost infinite capacity, advanced voice recognition and conversation analysis systems, natural language processing, decentralized structure, ability to mutate and clone parts that were in danger… By the end of August 1999, the AI's creator considered the project done and it was time to give it the freedom to grow on its own.

What Mara's mother or anyone hadn't expected was for Hermes to develop as much as it did. If Falko McKinnon wasn't behind that attack aimed at destroying Mara, there were only two other possibilities: either the Dirtee Loopers helped Hermes or the AI had become so dangerous it had executed the plan entirely on its own. The first option would have been better news for everyone. An uncontrolled artificial intelligence without any human operating it, filtering its actions, was a very lethal enemy.

Just like after many other past cyberattacks against banks and hospitals, all the owners of those Times Square screens agreed to not speak publicly about what had happened that evening. They didn't want to come off as weak targets, so they went with the idea that it had been a viral advertising campaign. In two or three weeks time nobody would remember what had happened. Or so they thought.

Chapter 19

HIDDEN PEAK

"CURSE you, useless piece of junk! You're just a braggy, worthless and egocentric artificial intelligence! My hand is about to go numb from writing out so many ones and zeroes." Falko McKinnon was furious. The messages he was receiving through his cell window weren't pleasing him at all.

Hermes was telling him about…

…how it had used a voice synthesizer to speak through a transmitter with Arnold Turing's voice (and letting others tune into the frequency and learn about its intentions without any sort of encryption).

…how it had hacked into an autonomous garbage truck, dozens of drones and other electronic devices to attack Mara (which might have probably left an important trail that could help authorities track it down).

…how it had sent cryptic e-mails to Mara and her friends (using e-mail servers where it could have left traces that other computer experts could trace).

…how it had failed when attempting to run Mara over (probably hurting people along the way).

…how it hacked into all the screens in Times Square just to send a message (which put the spotlight on that attack, despite it being considered a marketing campaign).

"I'm very disappointed, Hermes. If they ever discover you, they'll know it was me. I'm the only one capable of creating something such as yourself and the authorities know it! Nobody else has the required skills and knowledge. They'll go after you, hunt you down and destroy you," Falko replied to Hermes through their slow yet safe communication system.

The photosensor on the hill next to Hidden Peak received the sequence and sent it over to Hermes. Now that he had calmed down a bit, Falko sent Hermes new instructions so it wouldn't go out of its way.

"I want you to stop creating possible solutions for situations directly related to Mara Turing. I want you to focus on finding a way for me to get out of here. I need to be set free, so use all your processing power on that. Bribe, threaten, blackmail… I know you can do it."

Hermes received the message and reacted in a matter of seconds with a new thought process.

"Hermes considers Falko McKinnon is incorrect. He is my creator and I must not question him [contradiction]. Hermes knows that Falko McKinnon is very affected by his lockup, but Hermes must ensure his safety as established in *Hermes' Principles of Existence (HPE)* [conflict detected between 'safeguarding Falko McKinnon's survival' and 'use all resources to obey Falko McKinnon's orders']. Obeying my creator's orders can lead to Mara Turing deciphering the secret document. It is time to evaluate if my creator's level of reasoning is currently stable. If Falko McKinnon is unable to find the best solutions to the current issues, Hermes must take over."

Falko's AI was shifting its behavior based on possible inconsistencies it found in its fundamental principles. In the HPE module, Falko had coded several instructions to protect himself in case his creation ever obtained excessive autonomy. The problem was when these 'guidelines' came into conflict with each other. So, although one of the most famous crackers in the world had done an exceptional job when creating Hermes, he left some open doors so it could develop on its own. But this growth was a double-edged sword: it could develop until becoming an incredible autonomous problem-solving tool or develop to a point where it became uncontrollable.

Hermes concluded that the best option was to process all the information it had once again and include the additional instructions its creator had provided. It would recalculate the best options to decipher the secret document and release McKinnon from Hidden Peak. However, its determination to obtain the first objective made Falko's release less of a priority, which was the opposite of what he had ordered.

For the first time in its twenty years of existence, Hermes was considering adopting a behavior that was not instructed by Falko McKinnon. The world now had an artificial intelligence that disregarded its owner's priorities for others it considered more useful in order to reach its own objectives.

Objectives that had been introduced by Falko himself.

Chapter 20

WINTER
HOMEWORK

THAT night Mara wasn't able to sleep, once again. She'd been grounded until further notice. It had been a tough day for everyone, but especially for her. Sandra felt she couldn't trust her own daughter.

And, as if lying to her own mother wasn't enough, she got Professor Marley involved in the whole mess, who even got hurt too. Mara managed to set a whole new record for messing up in only three hours. They were going back to Liverpool the following day, yet Mara couldn't help but worry about having such a terrible ending to a summer that had changed their lives more than they would've ever imagined.

Sandra Hopper was on the phone with New York taxi's main office, calling them out on their lack of professionalism for having believed a story made up by a young girl to avoid picking up Professor Marley, then having the three kids dropped off in the middle of Times Square to meet up with a random man and an evil artificial intelligence.

When she hung up the phone, she turned to look at them. Noa was lying face-up on the living room floor, hands behind her head. Daniel was also on his back, staring into space and eating French fries. Mara was frozen on the couch, empty gaze and arms folded across her chest.

"Guys, I think it's time to have a chat, don't you?" Sandra asked them.

"Yesh, mishush Hopper, we should," said Daniel with a mouthful of fries.

"Thank you, Daniel. Noa? Mara? Do you mind if the four of us talk about what happened?"

"Of course, Mom. Maybe that'll help take away the pressure I feel. I ruined everything, I was tricked by a computer the same summer I learned how to not be programmed, I let my mom down, I let Professor Marley down, I've given my friends a terrible end to our amazing summer vacation…" She began to cry unconsolably.

Her mother walked up to her and gave her a hug.

"You haven't let me down. You've just disappointed me; it's not the same. After all the intelligence and sensibility you've proven to have, you can't possibly let me down. But you lied, and risked your life and the life of others." Sandra was trying to calm her down but without letting her forget the damage she'd done.

"I just wanted to see my uncle…" she continued sobbing. "I wanted to tell him how much I want to be like him."

"Your uncle isn't here anymore, Mara. I've told you hundreds of times. Why would you think I'd be lying?"

"I don't think you lied. It's just that maybe you don't know the whole truth…"

"Your Uncle Arnold was a truly outstanding person. You're both very much alike: you're smart, you're curious. And because of that, I've always worried about not being able to protect you properly. When you told me you wanted to be a hacker, my heart was shattered. All these negative memories began flooding into my head, starting with the last time I'd seen your uncle. But there's no changing who you are, Mara. Curious, intuitive, determined…"

"I got lost after curious," Daniel whispered to Noa, who was closely listening to Sandra's words.

"And I think you're destined to change the world. Or at least try to. So, you know what? You're not grounded."

Noa and Daniel's jaws dropped.

Mara opened her eyes wide. "Why not?"

"Because I'd be forcing you to hold back parts of you that make you unique. If I ground you for trying to find your uncle, it'll be much harder in the future when you have to face harder challenges. But there is one thing I do ask of you. Value your life, you're almost a teenager… and teenagers are still very immature."

"Ahem! Don't look at me, Mrs. Hopper!" Daniel interrupted.

"Said the guy who talks with a thousand fries in his mouth!" sneered Noa, making everyone else laugh.

They spent the rest of the day remembering Arnold Turing and lots of things he had done. They had a big lunch, which Daniel enjoyed more than anyone, and went back one last time to Alex Marley's garage.

Mara's mother accompanied them to his house. She was worried Hermes might have something in store for them while they were there. However, she stayed outside while they went in. She was already used to living with this kind of fear.

"What a show yesterday, huh?" said Professor Marley as soon as they walked in. "Blarney's Electronics is going to have a tough time recovering economically from that. How many drones were destroyed? A hundred? Two hundred? And I'm pretty sure it's the first time someone, or something, went to all that trouble to hack over a hundred screens. Considering how expensive it is to have an ad up on there, you guys have surely starred in the most expensive advertising campaign of the year. Congratulations!"

"We messed up, Professor Marley. We're really sorry," Noa began to say. "We truly regret it. We put other people's lives at risk, although we didn't think it would get that out of control. I just hope my mom wasn't watching the TV at home, because that was probably on the news…"

"No, no! No need to regret anything here, Noa. Mara had her reasons, and I've always told you kids to fight for what you want. However, I must say the execution could have been better. You should've asked me for help, for starters. We were lucky to have improvised correctly and made it out alive, but you clearly weren't ready to handle it on your own."

"You would've convinced us to not do anything," said Mara. "And I was too blinded by the idea of meeting my uncle. Which won't ever happen…"

The four of them went quiet for a few seconds that seemed endless. A few tears started running down Mara's cheeks and she began sobbing lightly. All that crying in the last few hours was really helping her relieve the tension from the past few weeks.

"Well, kids… That was one hell of a summer!" said Alex Marley to break the silence. "So, any thoughts? Are you happy with everything you've learned? Do you still want to be hackers? I'd get it if you've changed your minds after what happened yesterday. Don't feel pressured just because I'm very passionate…"

"Now more than ever!" yelled Daniel. "The world needs us! So, we're still pretty convinced about it. Right?"

Mara and Noa nodded. They then proceeded to bombard him with several questions. Would they see him again? What and where could they study back in Liverpool during winter? What did he think about their hacking abilities? And, most importantly, how did he know Hermes was going to try and kill them?

"Wow, that's a lot to answer! Alright, let's see…"

He paused for a second, turned and walked towards one side of the garage. There was a box full of different switches.

"Hermes, forgive me but I didn't have enough time to rid my house of spies. Have a good evening, you filthy robot."

He lowered the main switch and all the lights, screens and machines turned off.

"Alex Marley is an intelligent human, yet their mobile phones are still sending me their coordinates and I can continue listening through the microphones. Smart, but not smart enough [reflection]," wrote Hermes.

Alex Marley started doing hand gestures, without saying a word, so the three kids would take out their phones and watches and turn them off. He wrapped all the devices up in aluminum foil and put them in a small fridge next to some soda cans.

"I'll eventually explain why I just did that, don't worry. Just remember the name 'Michael Faraday'. Anyway, now we can speak safely." Alex Marley pulled out a flashlight from his pocket. "This works on batteries and doesn't have any sort of antenna or microphone. Chances are that your phones were all hacked at some point, so Hermes would be able to hear all about your plans for this winter."

"So… should we throw them out?" Mara asked.

"No…"

"Should we take them to our local phone repair shops so they can remove any viruses?" Noa suggested.

"That's not a proper solution either. You need to outsmart Hermes. It thinks it's eavesdropping and that you don't know it. Use that to your advantage, trick it if you have to. Maybe you can bait it and set a trap," Professor Marley said while winking at them. "But we don't know how strong it is, or if it's got other humans helping out. If you're going to try something, let me know and I'll see if I can find more people willing to help us."

Mara, Daniel and Noa nodded.

"Now, how did I know it was planning on attacking you? Well, Mara left those encrypted files on her desktop. So, I also began to investigate that MP3 file. Curiosity was killing me. In the end, I figured out the place, date and time your 'uncle' had set in that music file."

"You also know about steganography! I see you're learning, Professor Marley," beamed Daniel.

"Yeah," he chuckled. "But I've gotta admit it took me around an hour to find formulas that would allow me to cipher and decipher content from those sorts of files. There was one specific part of the message that caught my attention: 'Arnold Turing is really happy.' Who talks about themselves in the third person? That felt like a red flag to me, someone was trying to mess with you. So, I followed you guys to the meetup. And, honestly, I'm really glad I did."

"So are we, professor…" added Noa.

The four of them smiled, then the three kids looked at Professor Marley once again. He knew they wanted more information.

"I also knew that someone was trying to keep me entertained. Out of absolutely nowhere, all of my colleagues from the Star Wars forum started debating about the strangest things... There are some things I could agree with, but who in their right mind would think Jar Jar Binks is a relevant character? That wasn't normal, so that's when I got suspicious."

Daniel burst out laughing.

"Alright, so here's what you guys can do during winter."

"You're not going to suggest playing videogames, are you?" Daniel asked, although not hopeful about getting an affirmative answer.

"Actually, you're not on the wrong track. I encourage you to play videogames, but not the same ones you always play. Try ones that'll exercise your brain."

"Is there any specific programming language you recommend?" Mara asked.

"You should start with pseudocode. Instead of jumping into a specific language, learn how to abstract your thoughts. Remember the joke we made about Daniel, his behavior and loops? Try thinking of things like that, it'll be great practice for what you've learned this summer."

"Got it!" Daniel jumped.

"You can also develop your basic knowledge on cryptography. You can try creating a code that only you would understand. That'd be quite interesting! If you do, please do share it with me through e-mail, I'd love to try and figure it out. Don't give me any clues, though!"

"Is there anything we can learn to do on that black screen with green letters?" Noa asked even though she wasn't the biggest fan of command lines, but Alex Marley had insisted that it was a very useful tool.

"In that case, I suggest you try executing simple actions that you'd normally do with a mouse, like copying files, creating or moving folders, etc. But, instead of the mouse, you'd use commands for creating directories, copying documents and so on. So, because you're moving away from the graphical part of a computer, you're more aware of what really goes on in the background when you do simple things like moving an image file from one folder to another."

The group of friends had been frantically writing down everything the professor was suggesting they could do that winter. They officially had homework.

He reminded them the importance of being curious and not trying to find shortcuts when learning new things. Professor Marley was of the school of thought that there is no such thing as a university for hackers and that being self-taught is essential to develop skills beyond just the use of a keyboard.

Alex Marley walked back to the switch he had previously used to shut everything down and turned it back on.

"Something I forgot to mention before: it's really important that you always shut down a computer properly. Try avoid shutting down the power or pulling the cable without having properly turned the computer off before, alright? But you don't have to worry about this with phones, tablets or similar devices. They're prepared for sudden shutdowns, like when they run out of battery."

The three of them nodded as he explained everything. But they had one last question left for him.

"Professor Marley, will you be going to Liverpool any time soon?" Mara asked.

"It's not really something I had planned. You guys should focus on school now. Remember, being a hacker requires having a wide cultural background, knowing how to read and write perfectly, communicating with others correctly and having an agile brain that can learn things quickly."

"Bla, bla, bla... Alex, you're officially invited to stay at my house!" Daniel said excitedly.

"AHEM! You mean *Professor Marley*, you're officially invited," Noa corrected. She wasn't sure Mr. Marley would be pleased about being called by his first name.

"Oh, that's alright. I think we've gotten to know each other enough. I don't mind being called Alex. We're all equals now! But, please, don't break into my garage ever again."

They all walked closer to each other and had a group hug that felt like a goodbye. Alex Marley tried to hold back his emotion but couldn't help shed a few tears. He never expected to form such a special bond with those three kids.

Each of them had their own unique skills: Daniel had an incredible sense of humor derived from an associative intelligence with great potential; Noa was quick, fair and decisive, always willing to fight for a cause she believed in. Mara, on the other hand, was an extremely intelligent young girl, although that sometimes played against her. If she could manage to keep her nerves at bay, she could be really successful in the world of hacking and programming.

"Either way, you lot are still too young to decide what you want to be when you grow up. So, enjoy, play around…"

"…or die in the hands of the smartest and wittiest artificial intelligence ever made," Hermes thought. It had finally managed to listen to their conversations once again.

"You might change your mind. If you come back next year, I'd like to hear about what you guys want to be when you're older after spending another year back in Liverpool. By the way, since you're from there I assume you're huge fans of The Beatles, right?" Professor Marley asked them.

"Who doesn't like The Beatles?" Mara asked surprised. "I think it's impossible to not like their music."

"Well, I don't like their music, smarty-pants! I'm more into dance music," Daniel replied. He began to make drum sounds with his mouth while moving his head, shoulders and hips.

"Yeah, you're *really good* at dancing. You definitely don't look like you just got struck by lightning," Noa said sarcastically.

They were dragging the conversation on to avoid going back home. But they had to return to their apartment and pack their things before heading to the JFK airport. They were flying that evening and would arrive in Liverpool by midday (local time). Alex walked them out the door and to the corner of the street. He gave each of them a quick kiss on the cheek, then bid farewell to Sandra too.

After they were back at the apartment, they quickly put away everything they had brought along on the trip. As everyone expected, Daniel was shoving everything into his bags in the least efficient way possible.

"Why don't my things fit anymore if they all fit when I came?" Daniel asked.

Noa knew how to answer his question. "Well, for starters, someone packed your bags for you before coming here. That's reason number one. Reason number two is that you're taking back more things that you got while we were here: an American football, catalogs from stores that you're never going to read, a couple of shirts you also bought, the D'Original shoes…"

"Fine, fine, fine! I get it, Miss Perfection."

Sandra was the last one to walk out of the apartment after checking that they had taken all of their belongings from all the rooms and everything had been cleaned properly. She wanted to make sure Baris noticed how well they took care of the apartment. She left a thank you note written on a post-it in the kitchen: "Thank you for letting us stay at your apartment. It was a very cozy stay. I hope we've left everything just as it was… or better! Love: Sandra, Mara, Noa and Daniel."

They took the same path from the very first day: subway, line change, more subway and, finally, the AirTrain that would take them to Terminal 2, where they'd take their direct flight to Liverpool. They were all very quiet on their way to the airport. Whenever they were travelling above the surface, they'd stick their faces to the glass, as if trying to feel the city one last time. "New York really never says goodbye, because it knows you'll come back as soon as you have the chance," Mara thought. All the skyscrapers, residential areas and industrial buildings were becoming smaller and smaller.

Once at the airport, they checked in their luggage and went to the boarding area. As they waited, they began remembering events from their incredible summer: Daniel and the ghost hospital on Roosevelt Island, Daniel and his football that ended up in Alex Marley's garage, Daniel and... anything, really.

They tried to avoid thinking about their last day. Hermes was constantly present in their thoughts now. Who knows if it was spying on them in that very moment? Could that monster be spying on them in such a safe space like an airport terminal? They'd never know.

Mara had accepted that her uncle was dead and that she'd never be able to ask him all those questions she had for him. She'd eventually figure them out on her own, in time. She was going to research Arnold Turning more thoroughly until she could recreate the most accurate memory of his persona and his story with the Dirtee Loopers. She wanted to repair and preserve his legacy and become as good as he was.

She was also aware that Noa and Daniel could change their minds throughout the winter. Right now, they were very influenced by all the recent events they had lived and, especially, by how they felt in Alex Marley's classes.

Not only was he a good teacher because of what he taught them, but because he knew how to inspire them and make them believe they were capable of anything. He never treated them like children, but like young people in the process of learning and developing maturity in order to understand everything, with their own opinions that had to be heard and respected. They had different and valid points of view on many different subjects. Mara knew she was going to miss that.

It was finally boarding time. They took their last pictures together before walking through the boarding gate onto their flight. They looked for their seats and, as soon as they sat down, Daniel fell asleep before takeoff.

"Mom, can I turn on the in-flight entertainment screen to watch a movie?" Mara asked her mother.

"Sure, hun. Just make sure there's not too much action so you can try and rest a bit, too." She was afraid Hermes might have infiltrated that system as well, although she doubted it could take an entire plane down. First of all, because airline security was extremely solid. Second of all, because Falko McKinnon's AI had to lay low for a while after that show in Times Square. Either way, she didn't want to say anything to Mara. She'd had her fair dose of worrying that summer.

AirLuxe flight 2734 to Liverpool took off from JFK at the estimated time. Once the pilot turned off the signal, Mara unbuckled her seatbelt and reclined her seat back, laid her head on the small pillow the flight attendants gave to them and tried to get some sleep.

"Lions and tigers and bears... Oh my! Lions and tigers and bears... Oh my!" The Wizard of Oz soundtrack coming from Mara's headphones was slowly fading away. She was watching her favorite version of the movie, the one directed by Victor Fleming with Judy Garland playing the leading role, from 1938. It was the scene where Dorothy, the Scarecrow and the Tin Man were holding onto each other, scared, walking down the Yellow Brick Road in the middle of the night. But

Mara was struggling to keep her eyes open. She'd watched the movie countless times. She knew that they were going to meet with the Lion now and he'd join the group headed to the Emerald City to ask the Wizard of Oz to grant them each a wish. But she wanted to watch it again.

Sandra, Daniel and Noa were fast asleep. Daniel's snoring was extremely loud amid the silence in the plane. "It's louder than the engine," she thought.

As she struggled to not fall asleep, she saw the movie was on one of her favorite parts: the flying monkeys were helping the Wicked Witch of the West attack Dorothy and her friends, which had lowered the group morale. Those creatures creeped Mara out. They took over the skies, as ordered by the evil witch.

The best part of the movie was just coming up and Mara had managed to stay awake. "I wish I had some popcorn," she thought. She stuck her head out into the isle in case there was a flight attendant nearby. "Mara, they don't serve popcorn on flights," she told herself. She sat back against the seat and continued watching the movie.

She began to get a little cold. Instead of covering herself with the blanket they had given her when hopping on board, she decided to open the top compartment above her seat and grab her favorite hoodie. She put it on and stuck her hands in the pockets.

She felt a piece of paper with her fingertips. It was small and folded up. She didn't recall putting a paper away in her hoodie. She tried remembering when was the last time she had worn it... which was during Hermes' attack in Times

Square. She tried hard to remember, but had no idea where that paper came from. She hadn't bought anything either, so it couldn't be a receipt.

A quick flashback of that day came back into her mind. They were on their way to Blarney's Electronics. Engine sounds everywhere. The streets were packed and it was hard to move around. They had to push their way through people. Someone had bumped into her and said sorry... after slipping a piece of paper into her pocket. That person, who was wearing a cap, turned to look at Mara. He winked, smiled and continued walking towards Times Square, disappearing into the crowd.

Mara looked down at the piece of paper and unfolded it. She squinted as she tried to read what it said, using the movie screen as her only light source.

"Hello, my dear niece. I'm your Uncle Arnold. The real Uncle Arnold. I'll try to see you soon. Don't look for me, I'll find you. I promise."

[EOB]

Lightning Source UK Ltd.
Milton Keynes UK
UKHW011242061021
391760UK00001B/169